ARCHLORD of EXILE

by

Kate Stevens

3AM
PRESS

This novel is entirely a work of fiction. The names, characters and incidents portrayed in it are the work of the author's imagination. Any resemblance to actual persons, living or dead, events or localities is entirely coincidental.

Title: Archlord of Exile | Kate Stevens

Description: First edition | 3AM Press

Identifiers: ISBN 978-1-990551-09-3 (e-book) | ISBN 978-1-990551-11-6 (paperback)

Subjects: BISAC FICTION / Romance / Science Fiction

Cover art by Sonata Creates

Cover typography by oliviaprodesigns

CONTENTS

About the Book

For thousands of years, the Sollirians abducted children from their homeworlds to fuel their magic.

Inez would know. She was one of them.

Like other star-maids, she was tethered to an archlord, Rylec. Unlike other star-maids, she fell for him, and he helped her escape.

Three years later, Inez can't forget Rylec or the people she left behind. Unable to return to Earth, she's started smuggling star-maids out of Sollir on unsuspecting intergalactic cruise ships.

Then, a sudden knock at her cabin door shatters everything. It's Rylec, her former archlord — and current *husband*, a pesky detail she tried to forget.

Exiled for helping Inez flee, Rylec is now determined to

bring her back to Sollir. Inez swore she'd never be his star-wife again, no matter how she craved his touch.

But Rylec will risk everything to claim her once and for all...

Author's Note

Archlord of Exile contains the following major tropes and potential triggers.

Tropes: enemies to lovers; forced proximity; second chance romance; forbidden love

Triggers: explicit sexual content; swearing; gore and violence, including death; forced captivity and kidnapping; references to child abuse; pregnancy and childbirth; and sexual assault (flashback and off-page).

Steam Level: Steamy

If you don't like LGBTQIA+ characters in your stories, my books aren't for you.

CHAPTER I

"The weather on Janus must agree with you, Rylec." A sly voice cackled, sending shivers through the darkness at the edges of the council chamber. "You look so... tan."

Rylec gritted his teeth, but kept his hands behind his back. An hour ago, Rylec would've assumed Naccius's comment was about the layer of dirt and sweat adhered to his skin, but servants had hosed him down after collecting him from the living hell that was Janus. Despite the moon's harsh sun, he remained as pale as the snowy mountain he was born on. All that had changed were his horns, the crystal texture brightening from white to gold. Though he had lost all privileges when he lost his position, Rylec shot Archlord Naccius a glare darker than the shadows twisting around the blonde male.

The archlord's smile split into a predatory grin. He crossed one leg rather dramatically and propped an elbow on his chair's stone armrests. "What do you think, Kratos?"

"That we should kill him." Archlord Kratos paced the length of the space between the stairs to his seat and Rylec's prisoner box. The male's wings ruffled with his energy, his clawed thumb stroking the hilt of his dagger. "My vote hasn't changed."

"We can't kill him." Archlord Eliaz's stern voice brokered no argument. The leader of the Tertian Council—once Rylec's greatest ally—tapped his jeweled fingers at a steady pace.

Naccius didn't sit any straighter, nor did Kratos stop his pacing, but both banished their thoughts of murder. Rylec could tell. They had no other reason to look so disappointed. Rylec's lip twitched. He couldn't help himself. "How kind, Eliaz."

Eliaz's glowing blue eyes narrowed almost imperceptibly. The archlord didn't have wings or horns or claws like most Sollirians, but he had some of the strongest magic Rylec ever had the displeasure of encountering. More than one of their training cohorts had overlooked the glow of his eyes and faint blue tinge of his skin and assumed his Sollirian blood was too diluted for magic.

He had never learned what happened to their bodies.

"Can we get to the point?" Archlord Severin was a hologram in the Tertian Council chambers. He most likely stood on their homeworld, summoned by the Empress of Sollir to interrogate prisoners. The male didn't have to do much more than stare to bring someone to a tearful confession. His pure black eyes marked him as a soul eater, a rare and terrifying bloodline.

But if Severin was on Sollir then the empress was involved and nothing good would come of Rylec's return to civilization.

He faced Eliaz. "I agree with Severin. Why am I here?"

The council chamber dropped into a heavy silence. Naccius picked at his sharp nails, Kratos paced faster, and Severin continued his dead-eyed stare. All waiting for Eliaz to deliver the bad news.

Eliaz had said *they* couldn't kill him. That didn't mean he wouldn't die today.

If the empress decided that was his fate, then so be it. He'd go to his grave without regret. It was all worth it to see her smile, rejoicing in her freedom.

Rylec leaned back in the box, crossing his arms across his broad chest. "Spit it out, Eliaz."

The archlord tapped the large ruby on his pointer finger. A hologram lit up the chamber, the glow lighting the high-domed ceiling and tinting the white stone a pale blue. Rylec instantly recognized the map of the Sollir Empire. Sollir itself sat next to their system's sun, but Rylec skipped past it and a dozen other worlds to the edge of the system. Tertia marked the edge of their empire, with Janus as a tiny ball of rock stuck in its orbit.

Rylec cocked a single brow. Why was Eliaz showing him a map every Sollirian child knew? He had spent the last three years on Janus in exile but living on the inhospitable moon hadn't damaged his memory.

A dotted line appeared, marking a path right above Tertia's orbit. Eliaz lazily waved a hand at it. "In three hours, an Earthling cruise ship will pass over Janus. I need you to infiltrate the ship and capture four targets."

Rylec smoothed the crinkle in his forehead the moment after it appeared. "What use does the empress have for Earthlings? Outside of the empire, we're little more than boogeymen, a half-forgotten nightmare told to scare children."

"I guess capture wasn't the best choice of wording." Eliaz flicked his ruby again. The hologram changed. "Retrieve, then."

Rylec's insides went cold. Four faces stared back at him. He didn't recognize three of them. His entire being focused on the fourth.

It wasn't the same picture they had posted across the empire after her escape. No, she was a few years older, her dark hair longer and the expression in her green eyes sharper, harder. In place of the purple star-maid robes she had always worn on Tertia, she dressed in a tight black jacket and matching pants. The sight of her sparked something he thought was long dead inside him.

With one look—from a splotchy security camera, no doubt—the fire within him flared into life.

Of course it did. She was his wife after all.

Rylec lost the smile playing on the edge of his lip, a growl rising in his chest. "No."

"The star-marked are property of the Sollir Empire, Rylec. The empress wants you to get them back." Eliaz stood from his high seat and strolled down the steps to the main floor. "Over the last two years, this operation has smuggled a dozen star-marked from us. They haven't returned to their homeworlds, and we haven't located their base of operations, but if enough of them band together, it will become a problem for us. We have the advantage of technology and magic, but we cannot erase the minds of an entire galaxy if they decide to reveal our existence. If the star-marked tell other civilizations about us, they will resist our beacon that makes them turn the other way when they get too deep into our space." Eliaz stopped before the prisoner's box and leaned forward. "We will then have no choice but to kill them all and terraform their planets, starting anew. But the empress has assured me she will pluck your star-wife from their ships and torture her to death first."

Rylec jerked forward with a snarl. "When I see you next—"

"—you'll have your wife and her newest escapees in chains, ready to be delivered to the Star Temple for re-education." Eliaz's glowing eyes held no mercy. He twisted his ring, turning Rylec around right as the doors to the chambers opened. Two guards wearing the star crest of the Sollirian Imperial Crown marched in. Rylec hide his flinch. For years, the crest had shown a vibrant valdi bird, but now the image displayed a white snake, crushing the bird's body. Suffocated just like his father, the former emperor.

Then two smaller figures entered, fracturing the memory of Oriel's shattered body. One was an older Sollirian female with stark white wings. The other... a small child in a pale gown, with dark hair, the greenest of eyes, and two crystal-specked, gold horns.

She was the spitting image of her mother.

Rylec's chest wrenched, threatening to tear his heart in two. Soriya was a child in a cradle when he last laid eyes on her. His own crystal-specked horns flared with a spark of light as his magic rose within him. The box at his feet rumbled. None of the other archlords reacted to the tiny tremor. With the cuff on his wrist, his magic was a fraction of its true might and not a threat.

If he hadn't been chained... Rylec clenched his fist. Eliaz wouldn't even have the chance to control his mind before he would crush the male into little pieces. And he wouldn't stop there. Not until the streets of the empire flowed with blood.

But all Rylec could do was stare.

Eliaz settled at his side and leaned closer to whisper. "Your choice, Rylec. Which one will suffer: your wife or your child?"

CHAPTER 2

"Welcome to *Paradise*, where all your greatest dreams will come true among the stars. On our fifty-day cruise, all the luxuries of *Paradise* will be at your fingertips, from our indoor rainforest spa to forty-five dining halls..."

Inez gently nudged Hannah's shoulder, the first of her charges gaping at the *Paradise* cruise ship's bright atrium. The flashing lights, the dancing holograms, the blast of music... It was a lot to take in, but today was day twenty-six of the cruise. All the guests of the *Paradise* had long gotten used to the abundance of their accommodations.

Hannah snapped her jaw shut, but her dark eyes remained wide. "It's like Las Vegas on a spaceship. My family drove through it once on a trip to the Grand Canyon." Her face shuttered. "It was the last trip I went on before my abduction."

"Maybe someday you can see it again." Inez matched her pace to the young star-maid's. Behind the two of them, Rana and Astro followed, both a thousand times more successful at keeping their emotions off their faces. Neither were Earthlings—Rana a feathered Guroverian and Astro a blue-scaled Herkleian—so the *Paradise*'s Vegas theme probably didn't trigger anything more than a headache.

With her three charges accounted for, Inez continued her scan of their surroundings. In twenty-four hours, they would be out of Sollirian space, but until then, she kept a watchful eye. In her two years of smuggling star-maidens out of the Sollir Empire, no hunter had ever caught her or one of her charges. There had been a close call a year back, but thanks to an airlock and some minor hacking, no one had gotten hurt.

Besides the Sollirian hunter that is.

As they crossed the atrium, the sleek check-in desk staffed by a dozen humans in tacky red uniforms came into view. A few of the receptionists dealt with customers, but most of the *Paradise's* guests were too busy drinking and partying and gambling at this hour to require assistance.

Hannah stumbled mid-step. "What are you doing? If they scan us, they'll know we're stowaways."

Inez stopped. Rana and Astro halted before they could run into the two women. Inez put a hand on Hannah's shoulder, twisting her so she spoke with all three of her charges. "Hannah, I know you don't know me, but the Star Network vouched for me, did they not? I was once like you, fleeing for my life. I was terrified. I didn't trust anyone. I get that. But I've done this a hundred times. Since I escaped, I have dedicated my life to rescuing my brothers and sisters. I won't let you down."

"But—"

Astro put a scaled hand on Hannah's shoulder and said in his deep, rumbling voice, "Everyone on this ship thinks we're flying through uninhabited space, sister. They will believe whatever lie Sister Inez tells them. To them, there is no alternative."

Hannah nodded, but her eyes flickered anxiously between the receptionists, the roaming guests, and the patrolling security droids.

At this rate, Hannah wouldn't last another ten minutes. Inez worried about Rana too. The last of her charges hadn't said much in the twenty-four hours they had known each other. When they had switched from their violet star-maid robes to the clothes Inez had stashed for this mission, Inez hadn't missed the crisscross of scars cutting through the Guroverian's feathered back. All star-maids were slaves and property in the Sollir Empire, but some masters were crueler than others.

Inez needed to get her charges out of the public eye, stat.

She faced Astro. "Stay here. Don't let either of them wander away from you."

Astro nodded solemnly.

Inez spun on her boots and strutted for the concierge desk. But she didn't walk in a straight line—she stumbled, listing slightly to the left with a sloppy smile on her face. When she reached the desk, she bumped straight into it and flung her arms across the top, linking them to the edge where the holo-screen floated. She wrapped her hands around the edges and held on, like if she loosened her grip she might fall smack-dab on her face.

"Uh, hi, hi." She waved messily at the nearest receptionist, who approached with a cheery grin. "Hi-yas. Can you help me? I—" she thrust one arm out, the one with a holo-wristlet in the place of a watch, and nearly flopped to that side "—I think my door code isn't working. It won't let me into my room."

The receptionist flicked at the holo-screen. "Let me help you with that, M s.—?"

Inez ignored the question. "Like what am I going to do if I can't get into my room? Roam the hallways forever?" She let out a long, dramatic sigh. "I have to pee sooooo badly."

The receptionist's smile didn't twitch in the slightest. He was good. "If you give me your name, Ms—"

"Abigail Jones. That's A-b..." I squinted at my hands, counting off the letters. "I..."

"That won't be necessary, Ms. Jones. I see you in our files." The receptionist moved from screen to screen. Inez had fought back nerves the first time she played out this con, but the Star Network's hackers hadn't failed yet. "I apologize for the inconvenience. I can reset your door code. Your three companions will also receive the new code."

"Oh, good. That's so good." Inez blinked around the atrium blearily. Astro, Rana, and Hannah hadn't moved from the spot she left them. She made her eyes pass them. "That's so good. I should go find them."

"Can I help you with anything else, Ms. Jones?"

"No, no." She patted his hand, missing the first time and slapping at the air. "But thank you. You're so nice. So nice."

There. A twitch in the smile. No ordinary customer would notice, but Inez had trained for years to notice every slightest change in emotion. It was the foundation of a star-maid's training. "Have a good day and enjoy the bounties of *Paradise*."

"I will, I will." Inez pushed off the guest check-in counter and wandered back to her charges. No eyes followed her. She was just another drunk girl on the *Paradise*, destroying her liver without a care in the world.

Inez hadn't ever been so careless. Not since she was nine, at least.

When she reached her charges, she didn't stop walking. "This way."

They followed her like lost ducklings. Poor things. She didn't know much about their pasts, but her contact in the Star Network said they were all recent escapees. Inez remembered that fear. She had been convinced the Sollirians were going to find her for almost a year after she settled on Artema, a planet on the far side of the galaxy and a place of refuge for enemies of the Sollir Empire. Even now, within the empire's borders, an old fear gnawed at her gut.

And anticipation, too, an emotion she never admitted to her psychologist.

The closer she was to the empire, the closer she was to her daughter.

Inez pinched herself. She didn't let thoughts of Soriya distract her on her missions. One day, she would locate her daughter. Someone in the Star Network would learn something. She would make a plan.

It would succeed.

She entertained no other option.

Inez tapped the button to a transporter, and it dinged like an elevator before opening. The four star-maids squeezed into the square space. Within a minute, they were at their floor and within another, at their door. Inez waved her wristlet before the door's scanner. It clicked open to reveal a single-room suite, with two hovering double beds, a kitchenette bar, and a small circular table near a window overlooking the planet below.

Tertia. The planet she had once called home. Where her daughter was born.

Inez glanced away from the windows, moving to the side and letting her charges in before the door locked behind them. Hannah went straight to the bathroom, whereas Rana sat robotically at the table and Astro wandered the space, examining his surroundings. It was a tight space to be locked in for twenty-five days, reminiscent of the dorms in the Star Temple.

At least no one would rip them out of their beds every morning at dawn to run laps around the property.

Inez settled into the seat across from Rana. The other female's eyes were locked on Tertia. From above, the planet looked undeveloped, barren, but through the perception shield, a whole civilization lived and prospered. Thousands of star-maids served their archlords, sharing the power of their very life forces so the lords could generate stronger magic.

Inez wanted to take her charge's hand, but she didn't dare touch her without consent. "Can I get you anything, Rana?"

Rana's gaze flickered her way. She gave a quick jerk of her head.

Inez stood, planning to get the female a glass of water anyway. It had been hours since they left the Star Network base on Tertia. Surely they could all use a drink.

Inez plucked a glass from the kitchenette's counter.

Someone knocked at their door.

Inez's fingers slipped. She clawed for the glass, but it was gone, the cruise ship's artificial gravity dragging it to the floor. Inez flung out a hand—

The glass halted in the air and flew backwards into her grasp.

She stared. Rana stared. Astro stared. Hannah, who'd exited the bathroom at the knock, stared. Inez examined the glass like it held all the secrets in the universe. That was impossible. She hadn't moved an object with her mind since—

Inez dropped the glass. It shattered against the ground. "Fuck."

Hannah gripped the bathroom door frame. "How did you—?"

Inez pulled the kitchenette drawers open. Where was a sharp knife when she needed one? She settled on a fork and twirled it in her grip. The things she could do with kitchen utensils when motivated. "Get ready for a fight."

"A fight?" Hannah paled. "What are you talking about? How did you use Sollirian magic—"

Armed with her fork, Inez marched to the door and pulled it open. Rana scrambled from her seat and Astro pulled a small dagger from within his coat. Star-maids trained in combat in the event rebels attacked an archlord and went for their power source. Inez could thwart a hunter or two, but none of them were meant to fight an archlord.

Even if it was an archlord she knew.

Her eyes meet dark pools, a sharp contrast to the male's pale skin and towering white-gold horns. His nostrils flared like a beast scenting his prey. His strong jaw, the arch of his pale brows, the little curl at the end of his chin-length white hair—all unchanged. Archlords could extend their life a hundred years with magic. Had he found himself a new star-maid to drain in her absence?

But that didn't matter. Only that he didn't succeed, whatever his mission. Someone had dressed him in an Earthling suit, but he had ditched the jacket, unbuttoned the collar, and rolled the sleeves to expose muscular arms. Whatever he was here for, it required stealth. Inez raised her fork, her expression stern. His lip curled—a look that made her insides flutter—but it wasn't with the total confidence he carried when they first met. Something about him seemed almost... sad.

"Hello, wife."

CHAPTER 3

H *er.*

Rylec drank in the sight of his wife. Her dark hair and the flush of her skin. The way her eyebrows pinched as she glared at him. The bright green of her eyes. The curve of her body. His blood heated. Nearly three years had passed since he last saw her. He never thought he'd see her again. Smell her again, the thick floral scent of ikaias in the air. Everything in him strained to close the distance between them and touch her.

But Rylec liked all his appendages where they were and Inez would certainly cut something off if he got any closer. Even armed with a fork.

"Sollirian," one of the star-maids behind his wife shouted, grabbing at the first blunt object within reach.

Rylec flicked his fingers. All three of the star-maids froze, their bodies held in place. Sure, two of them had no intention of moving, locked in fear before he encased them in his magic. But Rylec couldn't risk this... abduction.

Inez clenched her fists, but her voice remained deathly calm. "Let them go. Now."

He wanted to heed her command. Wanted to pull her into his arms. Wanted to preserve the freedom she had gained outside the Sollir Empire.

But one thought pushed him forward.

Soriya.

The image of Soriya between those two Imperial Guards drenched him in fear like the icy rivers outside Lucian Manor, where he had trained with other future archlords. The headmaster loved nothing more than to throw his students in when they misbehaved. If they didn't climb out and the river claimed them, then they were never meant to be archlords, now were they?

Rylec had failed Soriya. He had failed his wife. When he had dropped her on a cruise ship just like this one three years ago, he had sworn he'd rescue Soriya from the empress's clutches and reunite the three of them. But he hadn't. Soriya had stayed on Sollir, raised among the palace's children. Rylec had been exiled to Janus, unable to leave the moon's surface or else be blown out of the sky. And his wife had apparently joined the same smuggling ring that rescued her. She had taken action. Rylec had only failed.

He couldn't fail again. Rylec had to protect Soriya. If his wife knew, she would make the same choice.

"I can't do that, Nez." He hooked one thumb into the ring of his belt loop and strolled forward. Inez shuffled back unconsciously before halting her traitorous feet. Good. He didn't stop his approach. The scent of ika-ias thickened the air until he was a breath away. Inez held herself still, her body a wall between him and her charges.

He leaned forward, his murmur a brush against her skin. "I really do apologize."

She swallowed, almost audibly. "For what?"

"For this." The anti-magic cuff he gently brushed over her wrist snapped shut with a buzz.

Inez jerked back as if she slapped him. He felt it too. As he'd approached the *Paradise* and his wife, the well of magic in him had grown. Even after years apart, the tether between an archlord and his star-maid didn't fade. The Star Temple had denied him a replacement—not that he would have accepted one—and he had gotten used to life with only his own power at his disposal. But Inez wasn't just his star-maid, a secondary battery of magical power for him to tap into—she was his star-wife. She had been tethered to him unwillingly, but he had tethered himself to her of his own volition. The connection between them wasn't one way. She shared her strength, and he shared his magic.

Of all his crimes, that one had pissed off the empress the most.

"Inez—"

"You dirty bastard." Her fist careened toward his face. Rylec should've expected it, but few people swung fists at archlords—even disgraced archlords. He shifted slightly to the left, but her knuckles grazed his chin. Pain ricocheted through his face. Star-maids certainly knew how to throw a punch.

Gods, he wanted to bend her over something and fuck her until she screamed. Nothing turned him on more than a fight.

Rylec twisted his evasive move into a smooth slide, leaning into the door frame and crossing his arms. His lip twitched further into a full-on smirk. It pinched at his sore chin, but Rylec didn't care. Anything to get a rise out of her. "I deserved that."

Inez's eyes narrowed and she lunged forward with a growl to rival Archlord Kratos. She wielded her fork like a spear. A punch he could take, but Rylec liked both his eyes where they were.

He reached out with his magic and halted her bones, stopping the movement an inch from his face. Rylec shuffled out of the door frame until her huffing breath tickled his skin. Another inch and he could claim her lips. He made sure to stare before slowly raising his gaze to hers. "Don't test your luck, wife."

She spit on him. "Don't call me that. You lost that right today."

"It's what you are." Rylec raised his hand and summoned a napkin from the kitchenette. He dabbed gently at his face as he circled his wife. He hadn't looked closely at the reports on her three escapees. A human female, a Herkleian male, and a Guroverlan female. None of them moved, but their gazes flickered between him and his wife. "Did your charges know that? That you weren't an ordinary star-maid, but a star-wife, a thing of myth."

"Don't talk to them."

Rylec grabbed a chair, twisted it around, and plopped into the seat. "I can't talk to them, can't speak to you. You have so many demands, wife."

"Why are you here, Rylec?"

He spun his finger, and she twisted around to face him. That was better. She deserved to look into his eyes as he told her about his mission. Gods, she'd hate him.

But once she learned about Soriya, she'd understand. After all, he had promised to take care of their daughter, no matter the cost. "To take you back."

Inez stared. Silence filled the cabin for three... two... one—

"Are you out of your right-fucking *mind*?"

Rylec repressed a flinch. She had always been a screamer. "Unfortunately."

"You piece of shit—"

Rylec pinched his fingers and his magic zipped Inez's mouth shut. She deserved the truth, but this didn't need to be any harder than it was. And he couldn't tell her the truth, not in front of her charges. Once the Star Temple got their hands on them, they'd reveal everything asked of them. Their fate was sealed, but he could still save Inez and Soriya.

He stood and crossed the space before his wife. He reached out, hesitantly, gently, until his fingers brushed her face. Shivers traced through his arm. He had missed her. Craved her. Not a night had passed without thoughts of her lulling him to sleep.

Though she glared, her pupils dilated.

She had missed him too.

"I have my reasons, Inez." He pressed the ghost of a kiss to her forehead, breathing in her scent. "For now, trust me."

"Rylec…"

He pulled back, staring into her beautiful face. "Yes, wife?"

Her green eyes went dead cold. "Fuck you."

Her knee jerked up. Rylec jumped back, pushing his magic back across her body. Even with a star-wife boosting his powers, he couldn't hold four people still, levitate his shuttle off the back of the *Paradise*, and keep the explosive he had planted in the engine room from going off. His grasp slipped, but he strained to reach, grabbing all the pieces with his magic—

The bomb ticked to 0:00:09.

Oh, well. Now seemed like a decent time to end the conversation. It'd give his wife time to process.

Rylec let go. The bomb started ticking down. Inez stumbled into his arms. Her charges raised their weapons.

Rylec wrapped his wife in his grasp. "Stab me after the explosion, will you?"

Inez froze, fork halfway to his balls. "The *what?*"

A distant rumble echoed through the cabin before everything went flying.

CHAPTER 4

I nez dug her nails into Rylec's shirt as the *Paradise* jolted, throwing bodies and furniture in the air. The lights flickered and the artificial gravity died. She tightened her grip, hoping her nails went straight through the thin fabric to his sculpted muscles. Maybe she'd get lucky, and the cut would get infected. He could choke on some pus for all she cared. He planned to take her and her charges back to Tertia—after he blew up an unsuspecting cruise ship filled with innocents.

But Rylec had never cared about that. Rylec cared about protecting what was his—his people, his territory, his power—at the expense of everything else. If he had to set fire to this ship to get what he wanted, that was what he'd do.

And what he wanted was to bring her *back*? It was a ridiculous notion.

The backup generators chose that exact moment to activate. Every thought fled her mind as gravity wrapped around her and Rylec. They had floated up to the ceiling, and the floor was a long drop away. Inez knew how to stick a landing, but she didn't need to use her training. Her star-husband wrapped those calloused hands around her waist and landed with perfect grace.

Her charges crashed to the floor with grunts and moans, the cabin a wreckage around them. The emergency lighting flickered on, followed by the blare of an alarm. But Inez barely noticed any of it, not with Rylec's hands on her.

A part of Inez wanted to lean into his embrace. Her heart had missed him. He was a bastard, a monster, an archlord. The system that raised him into power subjected her into servitude. She should have hated him. She wanted to hate him. But that didn't change their past. That didn't change the nights they spent together, talking and dancing and laughing. That didn't change the moment he had bound himself to her, making them partners instead of archlord and star-maid.

Rylec kneeled at her feet. "I tether myself to you, Inez. Willingly. Desperately."

She clutched his face, everything a blur through the tears. She wanted to scream with joy, but the servants outside Rylec's door would talk. "I love you, Rylec."

Inez hadn't let that memory resurface in years. She hadn't entertained any thoughts of Rylec actually. When he didn't return to her with Soriya in his arms, she feared him dead. But now that one memory returned and dragged dozens of others with it. Most of Inez's life had been terrible, all except her year of happiness, filled with love and laughter and Rylec.

"Are you hurt?" he asked, his voice a rumble in her ear.

Her stomach fluttered, but she didn't reply. She traced her hand gently down his side, almost like a caress. Rylec's breath hitched. He still felt something for her, then. But whatever it was, it wasn't enough to let her go.

Inez refused to be a star-maid ever again.

She grabbed the hilt of a dagger at his waist and pressed the blade to his throat.

Rylec stiffened. "There's no need for that, Nez."

"Isn't there? You just blew a hole in the engine."

"*Near* the engine."

Like that made a difference. Inez pressed until she drew a thin line of pale blood.

Rylec's lip flicked. Was he *smiling*? "The engineers on board will fix it within a day and the *Paradise* will be on its way—"

Another explosion rippled through the ship, knocking them all off their feet again. The dagger went flying from Inez's hand. She nearly slammed face-first into the floor but caught herself at the last moment. The cuff snapped off. She frowned at it. Anti-magic cuffs didn't just snap off. Had he put it on wrong? Intentionally? She rubbed at her wrist as the warmth of his magic brushed under her skin, but she didn't pull on the power. Not yet.

Inez pushed onto her knees and glared at Rylec, sprawled beside her. "And what was that?"

"A... miscalculation."

Gods, Inez wanted to throttle him. "What's your plan now, smartass?"

The alarm cut out suddenly, the silence momentary before a robotic voice said, "*Please follow the exit signs to the nearest escape pod terminal...*"

"Don't fret, wife." Magic wrapped around the both of them and they levitated to their feet. "We'll take one of the *Paradise*'s escape pods."

Like she planned on going with him. "If you think you can maneuver me and my charges down a hallway swarmed with panicking people, you'd be wrong."

"Hmm. Decent point." He flicked a glance at her charges, huddling together on the far side of the ruined cabin. "You're free to go."

"*What?*"

Rylec shrugged. "What a pity they died in the explosion."

Inez shuffled, putting her body between her star-husband and her charges. "You're not killing them."

"I didn't say I was. They can stay here for all I care." Rylec held out a hand and his dagger flew from the floor to his grasp. "Who knows? Maybe they *will* die in an explosion."

Inez twitched. She couldn't help it. Even if she somehow escaped this encounter, she'd need a year of therapy to make sense of it. "I thought you were here to retrieve me *and* my charges."

"I am. But the empress only cares about you."

Inez went cold. No, no, no. If she still had hold of Rylec's dagger, she'd have dropped it. Not the empress. Never again. Smooth hands trailed down her body, each touch wringing a scream of agonizing pain from her throat. Slitted, kaleidoscope eyes met hers over an innocent smile. Inez nearly puked at the memory.

Inez would rather launch herself from the airlock than encounter Empress Calanthe of Sollir ever again. What had happened to *her* Rylec? The male she loved would never return her to that monster. When the cuff snapped off easily, she hoped he hadn't changed. But her Rylec was gone. "And why in the world would I go with you? You plan on handing me over to the empress."

Those dark eyes slide back to her charges. "I'm not entirely opposed to their murders."

Inez's fingers itched for a knife. If only she had grabbed Rylec's blade off the floor first. But she wasn't used to having Rylec's magic. He only had time to teach her the basics before their escape attempt. On the other side of the galaxy, they weren't in close enough proximity for the tether to work. She lacked his instincts, honed since birth through brutal training.

Inez could, at the very least, thwart his attacks. But would it be enough to walk out with all her charges alive and well?

No, it wasn't.

She needed to take this fight elsewhere.

Rylec gestured gracefully toward the door, like the gentleman he clearly wasn't. The unnerving smirk still hadn't left his lips. Had he guessed her plan? Probably. Did he care? No. Not one bit. And that was what bothered her the most.

Inez glanced at her charges. "When you arrive on Earth, there will be someone waiting for you."

None of them replied, but she knew they had heard. They didn't trust her anymore, but once they arrived on Earth, they'd have no choice but to go with whoever the Star Network sent. There was no place for them back on their home planets. Any decent Sollirian hunter erased all memories of a star-maid from their family and friends' minds.

Inez straightened her shoulders and marched from the cabin.

Rylec followed behind her, his presence at her back sending a shiver up her spine.

This wasn't going to go well at all, was it?

CHAPTER 5

I nez remained silent as they entered the hallway. The lights flickered, throwing the catastrophe of a cruise ship into occasional darkness. Rylec stepped over broken glass, overturned vases, and an unnatural quantity of throw pillows. The haphazard furniture provided more of an obstacle course, but it didn't stop him from keeping pace with his wife.

Who still wasn't speaking to him. "What's the plan, wife?"

A vein in her forehead throbbed, but she didn't react otherwise. "What do you mean?"

"You have no intention of coming with me. I'm trying to figure out your plan."

She snorted. "I'm not going to tell you."

"I suppose not." Rylec linked his hands behind his back like they were on a casual stroll. "Perhaps you don't have a plan."

Inez stopped. "Rylec—"

He continued walking. "The nearest escape pods are right up ahead. Don't stop on my account."

She huffed, but a second later, was at his side again. "And what's your plan?"

He raised a single pale eyebrow at her. "My plan?"

"To get me to come without a fight?"

Ah. That. He pursed his lips. Rylec hadn't exactly had a plan when the Tertian Council dressed him in an Earthling suit, shoved him in a shuttle, and told him to be a good boy or else. He hadn't planned to fight his wife or leave her charges behind. But now that he had time to think, the answer was obvious. "The truth."

"And that is?"

They turned the corner to the stretch of hall before the escape pods. Three staff members in their gaudy red uniforms stood before the open doorways. Two of them calmed the line of impatient passengers, while the third walked from pod to pod, closing each set of doors manually. The *Paradise* was dead but the feeble-minded creatures of the Intergalactic Alliance thought this was uninhabited space. With nowhere to go, staying put and awaiting assistance was the best course of action if the ship wasn't going to explode immediately.

How annoying that it provided Rylec with yet another obstacle.

One of the staff spotted them pushing through the crowd and put on the galaxy's fakest smile. "I know this must all be scary, but there's no reason to panic—"

Rylec snapped his fingers. His magic jabbed out, applying pressure to all the right places in the neck. The man's eyes rolled into the back of his head as he collapsed to the floor.

Inez grabbed his arm. "What the fuck, Rylec?"

He didn't hear the rest of what she said. Someone screamed. The second staff member stared, wide-eyed. The surrounding crowd hadn't realized what had happened, but everyone was already on edge. Voices raised and elbows flew as humans and aliens in various stages of undress pushed forward. Nothing distracted like the panic of a crowd.

Rylec slipped one hand around Inez's shoulders and glided them through the horde. Limbs flailed in their direction, only to bounce off with a tap of his magic. With Inez at his side, it was effortless.

Even with her digging her nails into his spleen.

When they pushed through the thick of the crowd, Inez launched out of his arms. Her elbow ricocheted backwards in good measure. Rylec dogged it with ease and slipped around her to face the wall of escape pods.

"Don't you ever do that again."

"Or what? You'll glare at me?" Rylec surveyed his choice of escape pods. They didn't need something big. Enough room for two would do the trick... There. A pod the size of a closet, perfect for his purposes. If he gave Inez all the space in the world, she'd take it. So he wouldn't. "This one will work nicely."

Inez crossed her arms. "I'm not going with you. I'm never going back."

"Don't say never." Rylec leaned against the pod with an eye on the still-panicking crowd. He wouldn't allow anyone to get close, but that meant convincing his wife with non-magical means. "You were on Tertia yesterday. If I let you go, will you stop aiding escapees? If not, you'll have to return to Tertia eventually."

"Returning to save my brothers and sisters isn't the same as going back in chains."

He hooked a thumb into his pockets. "I don't see any chains."

"You cuffed me a few minutes ago."

"And they broke. I didn't bring a second pair."

She sighed. "The point is, I'm not getting in that pod willingly, so—"

Rylec crossed his arms, his pale muscles flexing. "Get in the escape pod, wife."

Inez crossed her arms back and glared. "Have you gone insane? You helped me escape. You told me to never come back, to move on, to live a great life. Why bring me back?"

Instead of answering, Rylec stepped into the escape pod and settled into a seat. As his long fingers buckled the seatbelt, his eyes found her once again. There was one thing he could say to get her moving. Just like there was one way for his family to get out of this alive and intact. He couldn't obey the Tertian Council and hand over his wife. Empress Calanthe would pluck her from the Star Temple the second she finished her re-education and Rylec would never see her or Soriya again.

To get out of this, Rylec required Inez's help. To get it, he needed to tell her everything.

"If you want to see Soriya again, get in the escape pod."

CHAPTER 6

I nez lunged into the escape pod and fisted a hand in Rylec's shirt. He only raised a pale, infuriating eyebrow in response. What had happened to the male she knew? He'd never threaten a child, especially his own. "If you hurt Soriya, Rylec, I will kill you."

He lifted his hands in mock surrender, but a hard glint had entered his dark gaze. "How little you think of me, Inez. Why do you think I'm doing all this?"

She tightened her grip. "Because you're a Sollirian."

"I thought we went over all this before, wife." He reached out, his knuckle brushing against her cheek. Inez shuddered. Gods, no one had touched her like that in so long. "The rest of my kind can rot in the four hells, for all I care. What matters is you and Soriya."

"Then why—"

Rylec leaned back in his seat and Inez automatically shuffled forward, drawn to him like a magnet. Any closer and she'd be straddling him. A spark of heat flared in her core.

It died with his next words. "The empress has threatened to kill Soriya if I don't bring you back."

Oh, look, my little dove had a baby dove. Inez recoiled from the words, from the concept. Of course. Empress Calanthe was many things, but kind was not one of them. If she wanted Inez back and had access to Soriya, she wouldn't hesitate to kill a child. Knowing Calanthe, she would make it hurt. Her baby would die screaming and Calanthe would make sure Inez knew every second of that torment.

Inez slumped into the escape pod's second seat. She didn't need to say anything. For Soriya, Inez would return to Sollir.

Her star-husband took his chance, tapping the screen and starting the escape pod's launch sequence. The seat buckled her into place as the engines fired, rumbling beneath her feet.

"Is she...?" Inez swallowed. She didn't want to know, but she needed to ask the question. Soriya's fate had haunted her every day since she left. "What happened to her?"

Rylec paused. For a second, Inez thought he wouldn't answer. But then he closed the space between them and took his hand in hers. His calloused thumb grazed across her palm. Inez shuddered. Gods, she loved his hands.

"After I left you with the Star Network, I went to find her." Rylec paused, swallowed, but his eyes didn't leave her. "She's been with Calanthe's court this entire time."

Inez closed her eyes shut, trying to banish the wave of nausea that swept over. How could this day get worse? Empress Calanthe *had* her daughter. She wasn't in some orphanage or being raised by adoptive parents.

Her daughter was in the monster's grasp right this second. Would it even be possible to save her without surrendering? The single scar on her back burned at the thought. The empress had whipped her a thousand times, but that first night, she had left a single gash unhealed. Inez could still feel the female's breath on her ear as she leaned down to whisper, "*Something to remember me by, little dove.*"

The pod's rumbling increased as it moved into position for launch. The movement jerked Inez out of the memory. Rylec watched her, waiting. With other archlords and scr vants, he had no patience, demanding answers immediately. But he had always waited for her. During those first few months as his star-maid, he hadn't asked a single thing about what she suffered at the empress's hand. He knew—everyone knew. But he didn't say a word about any of it until she was ready.

"And what about you?"

He paused. "I was sent to Janus."

Inez flinched. He didn't need to say any-thing more. Janus was a barren wasteland where traitors and prisoners went to rot. The loyal courtiers of Rylec's father, Emperor Oriel, hadn't lasted a month after Empress Calanthe dumped them there. The fact he was still alive spoke volumes.

Inez wanted to hug him close, but there was no room for that in the pod. Since Rylec had walked back into her life, Inez had been nothing but cruel. This whole time, he was protecting their family. Inez gazed at her star-husband, memorizing the strong lines of his face. Whatever happened next, she'd nev-er doubt him again. "Promise me you won't let the empress have her. You *will* rescue Soriya, Rylec. No matter what."

Those dark eyes didn't leave her. "I failed you once. I won't again."

"Good."

The escape pod dinged. "*Prepare for launch. 3... 2... 1...*"

Inez sat back in her seat, her entire body clenching. She hated space travel. No matter how many years had passed, she'd never forget that first night in the hunters' ship, huddled together with all the other children unlucky enough to have a star-shaped birthmark.

The pod launched.

The pressure pushed Inez's body back against the seat. Through the tiny window at her head, tubes and wires flashed by so quickly she couldn't even guess at what they were. She closed her eyes. Inez had seen the great black expanse of space enough for an entire lifetime.

Rylec's foot nudged her own. They couldn't speak, but Inez knew the touch better than words.

I'm here, star-wife.

Suddenly, the shaking smoothed and the light changed from bright fluorescent to a dimmer glow. Inez let out a long breath before opening her eyes to space. Stars twinkled in the distance, a beautiful and calming dance. Inez didn't hate the stars, no matter how many of her nightmares they featured in. It was everything else that made her queasy. The tiny escape pod, beeping and blinking. The *Paradise* behind them, the strobing emergency lights through the windows visible a mile away. And below it all, Tertia, an uninhabited swatch of green. If Inez's eyes could pierce the perception shields surrounding the planet, what she saw would look more like a sci-fi movie than a nature documentary.

And somewhere on that planet, the empress had Soriya. The throne of Sollir was planets away, but Calanthe wouldn't use a hologram for their reunion. The empress would want to touch her. Her magic wouldn't work otherwise.

Inez wouldn't stumble into that bitch's arms willingly. To save her daughter, she would return, but only as the last resort. "What's the plan?"

"Once we arrive on Tertia, we'll only have a few hours before they track us down." Rylec input coordinates into the escape pod's limited flight system. "I still have allies scattered throughout Tertia. I've been in contact with a Tertian archlord, too, though I'm not sure who. If we land outside Zareen in Archlord Nassius's province, then we might—"

Something hard thumped against the outside of the ship. The lights flickered. The pod spun. Inez grabbed for Rylec's hand. Through the windows, she spotted a piece of the *Paradise*, floating aimlessly. Something must have come loose in the explosion—

A light shot past them with a bright burst of color.

Rylec grabbed her hand. "Nez, close your eyes."

That bright light... "Was that a missile?"

Before Rylec could answer, the *Paradise* erupted into a burst of light. The ship cracked and crumbled. A huge chunk speared out, propelled by the force of the explosion. It rocked straight for them—

Everything went dark.

CHAPTER 7

"Inez?" Something soft and warm brushed her face. "Please be okay."

Inez clawed from the darkness, drawn by *his* voice. The voice that had haunted her for three years. She hadn't chosen to leave Rylec. They had planned to escape together, the three of them seeking sanctuary on Artema. Neither of them knew if the Artemans would accept an archlord, but they had to try. There was no place for them on Sollir with Calanthe as empress. Not for Rylec and definitely not for Inez.

In the end, it hadn't been an issue. Only Inez had escaped. And every night since, her body and soul ached for Rylec and their daughter. Ached for the life they could have had. Ached for the family she lost.

"Inez?"

Odd. His voice didn't echo in her head, the fragment of a memory. Inez pushed through the darkness. She clawed and ripped and tore like a wild animal, desperate for light and sound. As she neared the surface of her mind, the scent of smoke filled the air and the voice got louder.

"Nez? Fuck."

Strong hands gripped at her waist. Carrying her? Inez swayed with the movement. This wasn't a dream, was it? Inez had dreamed about Rylec's skin on hers, but she knew the difference, even after all these years. Those hands were real, not imaginary. She leaned into them, craving them. It had been too long.

A calloused thumb brushed against her lip.

That was all it took to jolt Inez awake.

She launched into a bright world on fire.

"Thank the gods." Rylec's arms tightened around her. They were in a forest, the foliage around them a rainbow of colors under a lavender canopy of branches. The Jaciel Forest. Maybe an hour away from the capital, maybe less. And given the smoke that wafted from their burning escape pod on the other side of the meadow, it wouldn't be long until they had company.

That calloused thumb brushed her chin, drawing her attention to his dark eyes. "Are you hurt?"

"No—" Inez's voice came out rough and patchy. She swallowed away the dryness. "I'm okay."

"Can you walk?" Rylec's dark gaze scanned down her body. There were a few tears in her clothes, but otherwise, she appeared unharmed. "We need to move fast. If we can get far enough away—"

"But we won't." Inez didn't need to glance over his shoulder again to see the smoke. Their escape pod had crashed in daylight and had been broadcasting their location ever since. Goddamn Sollirians. The *Paradise* had a thousand people on it, including her charges. Now they were all dead because of her. Tears pricked at her eyes. "We can't win by running away, Rylec. You know that."

Rylec's jaw clenched, but he didn't counter her point. He knew she was right. If she hadn't run all those years ago, the *Paradise* would still be in the sky.

"I don't want to waste any more time running." She reached out, a hesitant and gentle touch to his face. After how she reacted to him earlier, she wouldn't blame him if he turned her away. She had actually thought he'd hurt Soriya, his own blood and a child nonetheless. The comment must have stung.

Inez didn't know what would happen to them next. After the Sollirians captured them, it would be a battle to survive. But if Inez went off to war today, she wanted one last memory of her Rylec to keep her warm in the trenches. "Put me down."

Rylec gently lowered her to her feet without protest. Inez was tall for an Earthling, but her head barely reached the top of Rylec's shoulders when standing. She placed her hands gently on his chest. His breath stuttered out for a second before kicking into double-time. She'd always had that effect on him. Just like he had for her.

Inez had never experienced true pleasure before Rylec. At thirteen, every star-maid was paired off with another and locked in a room until they had 'done the act'—the clinical way the priests and priestesses referred to fucking. Inez had studied the art of lovemaking since age ten but experiencing it for the first time had been clunky and awkward.

That was the first time the temple forced her into a room, but certainly not the last. Girls. Boys. Star-maids like her. Volunteering Sollirians. Young and old. Before Inez turned eighteen, she had done it all. It was important for a star-maid to please their master.

But her pleasure had never been the priority. Not until Rylec.

Inez trailed her hand from his chest to the line of his neck to the angle of his jaw. His white hair tickled across her skin. The first time she went to his bed, he had wanted to prove he wasn't like other archlords. Those white curls had tickled across her thighs as he devoured her. For nearly a month, he refused to claim her with anything but his tongue.

"Nez," his voice came out as a growl. "It's not polite to tease."

Inez reached higher, knuckles drifting across the golden, crystalized exterior of his horns. In all her dreams, this was how she imagined them reuniting. Her hands gliding across his skin in passion instead of rage. She pressed onto the tips of her toes and whispered, "I'm not teasing."

Rylec's eyes widened, but he wasted no time. His arms went around her and lifted, drawing her closer to him. She threaded her fingers through his pale curls. Her legs wrapped around his torso, over a thick and throbbing heat. Inez gasped at the touch. Gods, she had missed him. She didn't want to miss him anymore, not when he was finally here. Not to take her back to the empress like she first thought, but to save their daughter. Save their family.

Their lips clashed together, like an anchorless ship against the shore. Violent. Passionate. Wild. Desperate. Inez opened herself and Rylec invaded, his tongue sweeping across her lips. She shuddered. Her body ached, a bright burning in her core. She wanted him inside her. Needed it. Now.

Inez broke the kiss. "There's no time, Rylec. I need you. Now."

His lips quirked. "As you command, wife."

Rylec pulled his hands from her hips. But Inez didn't fall, held up by his magic. Her husband shucked off his vest and shirt, stripping in seconds. Her mouth went dry. His pale white skin looked like carved marble over rippled abs and powerful legs. Inez had admired his body a thousand times and touched every inch. But every time she saw it, she couldn't help but marvel at his beauty.

Her eyes slipped down to the thick width of his cock.

Her heartbeat stuttered.

Inez reached forward to pull him to her—

Vines dropped down from the canopy above and curled around her wrists.

Inez gasped as they pulled taut, trapping her hands over her head. Her wide-eyed gaze met Rylec's, but the archlord only smiled wider.

"My hands will be otherwise occupied, I'm afraid."

Inez opened her mouth, but no sound escaped. It didn't have a chance. Rylec closed the distance between them and claimed her mouth. She moaned into his lips. His hands skimmed down her chest, parting the soft fabric. Inez tugged on the vine, but it held her tight.

"Faster," she murmured.

Rylec obliged, kissing down her neck to her collarbone. A warm spring breeze brushed at her skin as her shirt came undone. Inez gasped at the air on her skin, remarkably cold compared to the heat of his fingers. He kissed lower, to the swell of her breasts. His hair brushed her nipples and the buds instantly swelled to peaks. Inez shuffled, desperate for him.

Those dark eyes flicked up to her for a brief second. Rylec's mouth curved into a sharp grin. Her breath halted. His utter beauty never ceased to surprise her.

That wicked mouth closed over one nipple.

Inez's head fell back as a moan escaped her lips. His tongue swirled over her flesh, coaxing the fire within her. Gods, she just needed to... Inez jerked, rubbing herself against him. But it wasn't enough. She needed him inside her—

One of Rylec's hands slipped beneath her underwear.

His teeth grazed her nipple as his fingers sunk into her wet heat. Inez couldn't stop her cry. She buckled against him, but her hands stayed restrained. "Rylec, let me go. I need to touch you."

His breath tickled across her skin. "Not until I'm done."

"Rylec, I—"

With a final kiss to each breast, he traced a line down her belly with his mouth. As he moved, her pants untangled, slipping down her thighs. With a flick of his free hand, her trousers tumbled to the ground, followed by her underwear.

She swallowed. "Your ancestors would be disappointed if they knew how you used your magic."

"My ancestors fucked anything that moved. I'm sure they did worse." Rylec stopped his trail of kisses at her waist, but kept his head bowed against her stomach. He inhaled. Inez shuddered. He was breathing in her scent. He had always said she smelled like ikaia flowers. They hadn't been able to go on many romantic trips together, but he had once taken her to an ikaia field and claimed her among the petals. His exhale ticked across her sensitive, exposed flesh.

Inez's back arched. She was going to explode, and he hadn't even started. Had it always taken him this long to get to the point?

Rylec wrapped a hand around each of her thighs and spread her wide. His tongue flickered out. Inez clenched the vines above. He licked the length of her heat, drawing a strangled cry from her throat.

Her head smacked back into the tree, her body arching. "Rylec."

He didn't respond, too busy devouring her, but a growl rumbled up. It vibrated against her. Inez didn't bother to hold in her scream. This wasn't his castle with servants gossiping in the halls. If anyone heard, Inez didn't care.

His finger plunged into her depth. Inez hooked her legs over his shoulders. Her body jerked, riding his movements. Her husband. Her mate. No matter what happened, nothing could ever truly separate them. She was his. He was hers.

Forever.

Inez shuddered, a wave of pleasure sweeping her over the edge. She shrieked, wordless joy mixed with her husband's name. She never wanted to miss him again. Whatever happened next, they wouldn't be parted. They would succeed.

Inez would wake every morning to his lips on her body.

She couldn't entertain an alternative.

When she floated back down to reality, Rylec's dark eyes met hers. His tongue swept out to lick his glistening lips. She shuddered, the embers within her sparking to flame again.

"You're mine, Inez," he said, his voice a deep rumble. "No one will take you away."

CHAPTER 8

Rylec brushed a dark curl from his wife's face. The two of them had curled up at the base of the tree, Inez tucked into the crook of his shoulder. Her body fit perfectly against his, stark white skin against pale pink. A purple-veined leaf tumbled from the tree above them to drop onto the curve of her bare ass. He flicked it off, but his hand lingered. After years without her, he'd do anything to touch her one more time.

But they didn't have time for that. They wouldn't run, but they wouldn't surrender either.

Rylec pressed a gentle kiss to her forehead. "We should get dressed."

Inez drew lazy circles across his chest. "Are they close?"

Rylec had noticed the low buzz of engines a few minutes ago. His star-wife obviously had too. "Close enough."

Inez let out a long huff. "What are we going to do?"

"You were right." Rylec pressed onto one elbow, staring down at his beautiful mate. "We can't win if we run. Empress Calanthe has Soriya. She has an army. But Solliri-ans follow power above all else. If we stand together against her, we're stronger. They'll cuff me in the empress's presence, but they won't cuff you. You're nothing more than a star-maid to them. They'll underestimate you every time."

"Do you have any idea which archlord is on your side?"

Rylec snorted. "None of them are on our side, wife. But no, I don't know which one has aided me the last three years."

"I doubt it's Kratos. He's too blunt for espi-onage."

Rylec smirked. "I'd love to see his face if he heard that."

"I wouldn't." Inez shivered despite the heat of Rylec's body and the warm spring weather. "He once killed one of his servants by growing a tree right through them."

"I know. I was there." As Governor of Tertia, he had witnessed the worst of the archlords' behavior. But he hadn't stopped it. Rylec hadn't cared until Inez came into his life. "Let's not talk of archlords."

"But—"

Rylec put a finger on her lips. He didn't want those thoughts in her mind when the Imperial Guards carted them back to the capital. The archlords were cruel, yes. All Sollirians with magic and influence were. It was why Rylec didn't waste time considering which archlord was a potential ally. They might have helped him once, but there was no guarantee they'd do so again. Neither Eliaz, Naccius, Kratos nor Severin were one to risk their necks for others.

"It doesn't matter. We can't control their actions, only our own."

Inez swallowed. "They'll separate us."

"Our tether can hold our connection a continent away. When you see your chance, take it. I'll do the same."

"Rylec—"

He pressed a kiss to her lips, swallowing her complaint. Inez moaned into his mouth, relaxing under his touch.

He only regretted having to pull away so quickly.

"You're not a helpless damsel, Inez." He traced a finger along her bottom lip to her chin to the line of her throat. He outlined the little star-shaped birthmark on her shoulder. If she hadn't been born with it, a fluke of genetics, they would have never met. "You're a star-maid. Trained in combat and conversation, deadly with both a weapon and a word. The Star Temple beat you down to keep you subservient. Given what they taught you, they couldn't risk an uprising."

"I know, I know." Inez kissed his fingers. "But when I see Calanthe again, I'm so scared I'll become that helpless girl I was before you."

"You're not helpless, Nez. Calanthe is a monster. She enjoys breaking people down. You got away from her scarred but alive. You survived."

Inez's green eyes met his. "I survived."

Maybe if she repeated it enough, she would believe it. His wife had changed over the last three years, growing stronger and more confident. He loved her more than ever. Together, they would grow. There would be a tomorrow for them. "And we'll survive this. You couldn't fight Calanthe last time. You didn't have any magic. But you have mine now. Even without it, you've spent the last three years besting Sollirian hunters."

Before Inez replied, an electronic zing echoed through the trees. "Did you hear that?"

Rylec pushed to his feet and grabbed his pants. "They're close."

Inez was already throwing on her shirt. "We should run. If we're just sitting here waiting, they'll be suspicious."

"You're right." Rylec didn't want her to be. If they ran, the Imperial Guards would chase them. Knowing the empress, she wouldn't want them dead, but Rylec doubted they needed to be captured unharmed. If there was one thing Calanthe loved, it was pain. "They'll expect a fight too."

Inez slipped into her shoes and pulled her curls into a messy bun. A beam of sunlight danced across her face, brightening the green of her eyes and the amber in her hair. Gods, she was beautiful. Rylec couldn't lose her again. He stomped down the urge to throw her over his shoulder and run deep into the forest. The only way to win was to stand their ground.

Inez glanced up at him and frowned, coming forward to put her hand on his cheek. "Don't worry about me. You're right. I can handle myself."

"Still..." Rylec removed a dagger from his belt. "Take this."

She snorted, but tucked the blade's sheath into the back of her pants. "And to think, a few hours ago, you wanted this blade out of my hands."

"If you were planning on stabbing me, I still would. I don't care if you want to stab others. Stab away."

Inez drew her fingers across his face, as if memorizing him. Rylec grabbed her hand and kissed her knuckles. "I love you, Inez. I have since we met five years ago and I will until the day I die."

"I love you, too, Rylec. I never stopped."

A high-pitched tone blared through the forest. The Imperial Guard, announcing their presence. Inez pulled out of his arms but didn't let go of his hand. Rylec squeezed. Her green eyes met his black. A thousand things went unsaid between their gazes. Inez smiled at him, a grin of both hope and despair.

They would get through this. Rylec wouldn't fail his family twice.

"Rylec Vanoriel," an electronic voice blared through the trees. "Surrender yourself and your star-maid to the Imperial Guard of Empress Calanthe the First. Disobey, and we have orders to use force."

"Go now," Rylec said. "I'll draw their attention."

Inez didn't move. "We stand together. I'm not leaving you again."

Rylec wrapped her hand in his and brushed a quick kiss against her knuckles.

"Rylec Vanoriel," it started again.

"Yes, yes, I heard you the first time," Rylec shouted. "Pass along a message to your empress for me. Tell Calanthe to go fuck herself."

The horn cut off. Good. He had always found the Imperial Guard stuffy and annoying, even when they obeyed his father rather than his father's murderer. "We should—"

A blast flared through the meadow, throwing Rylec and his mate off their feet. Inez hit the grass and rolled. Rylec glanced up—

A guard dropped from the sky.

Rylec threw up a hand and the guard flung into the air. As they went up, Rylec twisted. The guard's body wrenched in half. Two other soldiers fell through the foliage, but Rylec flung their comrade's body at them. They crashed to the dirt.

Rylec flipped up into a standing position. Inez had already returned to her feet. She punched her knife straight through a guard's chest. Rylec grinned. What a bloodthirsty wife he had.

Eight more guards dropped from the ship above.

Neither Rylec nor Inez hesitated. She threw her knife and followed the path, knocking out an opponent with a twirling kick. When two guards raised their weapons at her, Rylec spun them around. Their laser blasts fired at each other, and they went down in a pile of seizing limbs. Rylec grabbed another with his magic—

Something hard knocked against the back of his head.

Rylec went to his knees. Another ship had arrived. Imperial Guards swarmed into the meadow, so many that he couldn't count them all. They rammed into Inez, tossing her to the ground. Rylec roared and rammed to his feet, but hands wrapped around his arms and tugged him down.

Rylec pulled on his magic—

Inez went pale. Shit. He hadn't yet recuperated from the *Paradise* and his magic was nearly depleted. But he couldn't pull from her, not when they both battled for their lives. Rylec wouldn't risk his star-wife. She needed her strength for their plan to succeed.

Rylec growled and struggled, but the hold was too tight without his magic.

An approaching guard pulled something from his belt. Rylec jerked at the flap of black fabric. A blindband.

The guard threw the fabric and it morphed, becoming almost gelatinous. It split into two, one splattered against Inez's face before the second hit him. It invaded his mouth and his eyes and his nose until nothing remained but endless darkness.

Rylec roared into the silence of his own mind.

CHAPTER 9

Six hundred and ninety-eight. Six hundred and ninety-nine. Six hundred and fifty. With each number, Inez breathed deeply, savoring the taste of air in her lungs. With the blindband still around her eyes, mouth and ears, her sense of smell was all she had left. Why the nanites invading her brain didn't suppress that sense too was a mystery. Probably because eliminating all senses would drive a person to madness.

The Sollirians didn't want her mad. And that was perhaps more terrifying.

Nine hundred and thirty-two. Nine hundred and thirty-three.

When a buzz sounded in the nothingness, Inez almost laughed in relief. Thank the gods.

The Star Temple had placed her in a blind-band before, as some archlord were wont to do. Neither Rylec nor the empress had ever placed her in one. It had been too long since her training. Her tolerance wasn't as good anymore.

Slowly, the world returned. The room was dim, quiet. Inez shuffled, the chair beneath her soft enough, all things considered. She blinked, clearing the fog from her eyes. A dark-haired male walked to the seat across from hers, tossing the blindband into the air in his left hand. When he turned and sat, Inez stiffened.

Archlord Eliaz's electric blue eyes pierced through her soul. They always had. Inez had never interacted with him, but as Rylec's star-maid, she had followed him to meetings, waiting in the antechamber with the other star-maids. Whenever the lords departed, only Eliaz had looked at each and every star-maid with that all-knowing, blank stare.

Inez tried to quiet her mind, but there was no point. Eliaz only needed to look at her to read her mind.

Inez broke eye contact, looking at the ground.

Archlord Eliaz tsk-ed. "Now, now, Inez. See that guard behind you? If you don't look at me of your own volition, I'll require his assistance." The archlord leaned forward, his chair creaking. "I'd much prefer it if we had a pleasant conversation."

Inez sighed, a long huff. There was protocol for this. If anyone in the Star Network found themselves in a mind reader's clutches, they were supposed to protect their brothers and sisters at all costs. Even if it meant their life. Inez wasn't chained to the chair, but the surrounding room was bare, intended for nothing more than interrogation. Under the table, flies buzzed around a drain. No blood stained the floors, but Inez knew what that drain meant.

Inez stared at it and didn't glance up.

Archlord Eliaz sighed rather dramatically. "Kain."

Footsteps pounded behind her before a hand grabbed her chin, forcing her face upwards. Inez slammed her eyes shut, gritting her teeth through the pain.

There was a slow tapping of nails across the table. "You're not going to make this easy, are you, Inez?"

"Fuck you."

Kain squeezed tighter, pain flaring through Inez's jawbones.

"That's enough, Kain." The patient tapping hadn't stopped. "If anyone can endure pain, it's our Inez here. Wait outside. I'd like to speak to the prisoner alone."

Kain didn't speak, but the hand on Inez's jaw disappeared. More footsteps sounded, followed by the click of a door.

Fabric rustled as the archlord leaned closer again. "You escaped with three other star-maids. Where are they?"

Rage boiled through Inez's chest. She hadn't had the chance to mourn the star-maids she lost. She couldn't, not when her daughter was at risk and the only way to her was through the empire. But she grabbed onto that anger and stoked the flames. "They died when you fired a missile at the *Paradise*."

"Hmm. But before their unfortunate end, did they escape, or did Rylec let them go?"

Inez snorted. It was so like a Sollirian to shrug off death. "Why does it matter?"

Eliaz went silent. Inez wanted to glance up, but she didn't dare open her eyes. She wouldn't take her life to spare the Star Network. Soriya deserved a life with both her parents. But she wouldn't make it easy for the Tertian lord either.

"Empress Calanthe is here."

Inez jerked, her eyes flashing open. Her own gaze was ensnared by glowing blue.

Archlord Eliaz's lips curved into a smile. His attractiveness lessened the wicked bite to it, but not by much. "There you are."

Gods damn him. "Calanthe is here?"

"She is. She wants to speak with you."

Inez had suspected the empress would be on Tertia but she hadn't been sure. "Then why am I not speaking to her?"

"The Star Temple tasked me with locating their missing property. Even the empress wouldn't dare cross the priests."

"Calanthe would dare."

The archlord shrugged. "I caught her in a good mood. She obliged this conversation."

Inez sharpened her glare. "Is there a point to this conversation?"

Her tone only made Eliaz's smile widen. "The Star Temple will be distraught to learn their property is gone, unrecoverable, but I don't really care. What's three lost star-maids? We have thousands more. What I really want to know is, did Rylec let them go? Did you beg him for their lives, or did he offer it without your input?"

Inez ducked her head, breaking eye contact. "Why does that matter?"

Archlord Eliaz climbed to his feet and circled the table. His hand settled on the back of her chair, but he didn't touch her. "Rylec is with the empress right now."

Inez flinched again. Calanthe had Rylec. Was she torturing him? He was a disgraced archlord, but still an archlord. Rylec and Calanthe had a long history. At one point, before Calanthe killed Rylec's father, they were almost friends. That might be enough to keep him safe. Momentarily, at least. The empress would kill Rylec and Soriya without a second thought, but she would wait until Inez was there to watch. Calanthe loved nothing more than an audience.

Inez refused to watch any more people die today.

She twisted, ready to tell Eliaz to go fuck himself—

The archlord leaned closer. "Tell me what I want to know, and I might be inclined to help."

Inez couldn't stop herself. She looked at him. "Why?"

"It doesn't matter why." Those blue eyes remained on her. Steady. Confident. Conniving. "But as everyone who lives on Tertia knows, I despise liars. If you tell me, I will assist Rylec to the best of my abilities."

That was true enough. In all her years watching Archlord Eliaz from Rylec's side, she had never witnessed a lie. Neither had her star-husband.

Was the First Archlord the contact Rylec had mentioned?

Those blue eyes stayed on her, reading her every thought.

Inez swallowed. "He let them go. I threatened him a few times, but I don't think that was why he did it."

"Hmm." Archlord Eliaz leaned back and examined one of his rings, leaving her to her own thoughts. "Thank you, Inez. You've been most helpful."

As if that was some sort of cue, Kain stormed back into the room. Inez straightened in her seat as the guard charged her. Rylec had been right. They didn't view her as a threat and hadn't put magic cuffs on her. But Inez wasn't helpless. She wouldn't reveal her skills with Rylec's magic now, but she also wouldn't go anywhere with Eliaz's guard without a fight.

The large Sollirian stopped at her side and poked her.

Inez stared. "What—?"

Eliaz waved lazily at her. "One to transport to the imperial guest chambers."

Inez jerked to her feet, but it was too late. The world around her faded as a tingle vibrated through her skin from the point Kain poked. Before she could even process it, Inez stood in a different room, in a different outfit. Her plain Earthling clothes were gone, replaced by a solid purple gossamer gown. The interrogation chamber had turned into a high-ceilinged sitting room with gilded molding and crystal chandeliers. Plush couches formed three sides of a square in the room's center, with a table occupying the fourth and final side. Beyond the table was a majestic, canopied bed.

Three figures sat around the table. Inez spotted Rylec first. He appeared mostly unharmed aside from some bruising and a few tears in his Earthling suit. No one had bothered to get him a new outfit. A silver cuff lined his right wrist. But even with his magic repressed, an archlord was a force to be reckoned with. Her star-husband wouldn't be sitting quietly without a reason.

A little girl with brown curls and white-gold horns sat beside him.

Pain lanced through her heart. Soriya. Inez knew in her soul. Her knees went weak, but she stayed strong and standing. Her little baby had grown into a beautiful child, smiling at the world around her. A pure happiness radiated from her. No one had ever harmed her or starved her or hit her. That was all Inez could have hoped for and more.

Soriya glanced at her. "Mama, we have another guest."

Inez inhaled sharply. Mama. The words she had always wanted to hear. Inez opened her mouth, but no sound escaped.

Someone else answered for her. "This is an old friend of mine, baby dove."

Inez's stomach dropped. That voice. She'd remember that voice for the rest of her life. Inez followed her daughter's gaze, her green eyes staring up in adoration at—

Empress Calanthe of Sollir smiled and raised haunting, kaleidoscope eyes to meet Inez's own. "Hello Inez."

CHAPTER 10

I nez barely noticed the cold stone floor as she dropped to her knees. Her gaze fixed on the empress. The petite beauty dressed in a gown of pale wisps, her white hair curled in perfect ringlets to her waist. Her horns were short, golden nubs instead of tall and crystal-ized like Rylec or Soriya's. Everything about her screamed innocent and weak, a fairytale princess in want of rescue like in the stories from Inez's childhood.

But those stories were so, so wrong. When the empress had selected Inez at her Star Temple, Inez had thought herself lucky. Em-press Calanthe appeared kind and gentle. She might use Inez to boost her own magic, but Inez had trained to endure far worse situations. She had squeezed her brothers' and sisters' hands, all of them vibrating with jealousy.

Hours later, when Inez had limped into her room stripped naked and bleeding, she knew she wasn't lucky. She had been tethered to a monster.

Rylec crouched in front of her. "Inez."

She focused on his voice and followed it out of the darkness swirling within her. Her eyes met her husband's. "I'm okay."

"Back to your seat," a guard said, hand slamming down on Rylec's shoulder. Her star-husband's eyes went flat. If their daughter wasn't in the room, the guard would've quickly been short a hand.

Rylec stood stiffly and returned to his chair, a black fire burning in his gaze.

"Come, sit with me, Inez." Empress Calanthe patted the seat beside her. "Rylec, Soriya, and I were just about to start tea."

Inez swallowed down her fear. Empress Calanthe had owned her once, but she would never own her again. She was here for Soriya.

Her eyes met Rylec's again. If only she could tell him that Archlord Eliaz might be their secret ally. Without him, their chances of success were low. Inez might surprise Calanthe with her magic, but they'd still have the Imperial Guards to deal with. They would retaliate unless Archlord Eliaz mobilized his own soldiers.

But Inez couldn't risk giving any of that away in front of Calanthe.

Who stood waiting, the smile growing on her lips.

Let the bitch think it was fear that held Inez back. Was she terrified? Yes. But she wasn't the broken girl the empress once knew. She had lived without her husband and daughter for three years. Nothing could be worse.

Inez straightened her shoulders and crossed the gilded floor.

Empress Calanthe pulled out a chair, her dainty hands on the backrest. Inez's skin prickled, but she sat, careful not to touch the empress.

Calanthe stood behind her for a moment longer than needed. The tension crawled up Inez's spine.

Rylec plucked his teacup from the table. "Stop posturing, Calanthe. You have us. Now tell us what you want."

The empress tsk-ed. "That would be quite rude, Rylec. Didn't your mother teach you better manners?"

"My mother didn't teach me anything."

"Oh, yes, that's right." The empress circled the table to her seat. "Your mother was a star-maid. I remember when my mother killed her."

"I remember it too." Rylec sipped at his tea in a rather dramatic pause. "My father gave my mother to your mother as an engagement present."

"And then your father gave my mother to me as *our* engagement present. Emperor Oriel was big on giving away his former mistresses to his new ones. It was one of the reasons I..." —those kaleidoscope eyes drifted to Soriya— "...castrated him before I killed him."

"What does castrated mean, Mama?" Soriya asked.

Inez repressed her flinch, but Empress Calanthe saw the reaction in her eyes. The monster smirked as she brushed a hand across the small girl's cheek. "I'll tell you one day when you're older. Did you know, baby dove, that this is where your Uncle Rylec first met our new friend here, my dear Inez?"

"I didn't, Mother."

Calanthe glanced up from the child, the cruel smirk growing. "Do you remember, Inez?"

Inez raised her teacup, forcing her hands to remain steady.

Inez clutched the bed's footboard, her head thrashing. The pleasure crested in her, higher and higher, but it wouldn't release, to the point that every touch hurt. When Inez groaned, it was half-pleasure, half-pain. Her mistress's whip cracked against her back, etching another cry from her.

"Poor little star-maid," Empress Calanthe cooed behind her, pacing the bloodied space before the grand bed. "Do you want me to release you?"

Inez swallowed. "Mistress, mistress, I..."

"Yes, star-maid?"

Her mistress loved when people begged. Whether she was whipping her or fucking her or whipping her while fucking her, Empress Calanthe wanted to hear the same words from Inez's lips. "Please, please, let me go."

Calanthe grinned. "Good girl."

She lashed the whip against the floor, ready to release Inez from this torment. The first time Calanthe used her magic on her to switch her pain and pleasure sensors, Inez had been glad every hit made her moan instead of sob. But now, tied to the end of the empress's bed, her clothes torn and bloodied and puddled on the floor at her knees, Inez wished she felt the pain. Inez eyed the bathroom door, craving a moment alone to wash what little shame hadn't been tortured out of her—

The door slammed open.

Inez nearly sobbed as Empress Calanthe jerked around. If Calanthe got angry, if she left to kill this poor fucker who stupidly walked into the empress's chambers, Inez would be stuck in the throes of pain and passion, unable to do anything but wait. Calanthe couldn't hold her magic on anyone else without physical contact, but Inez was tethered to her, a pathway between them active at all times. Calanthe would leave her squirming for hours.

Inez would be begging by the time her mistress returned, all to Calanthe's great satisfaction.

"Who dares disturb their empress?"

Inez shuddered at the tone, but whoever obviously entered wasn't that smart.

"There's no need for—" The footsteps faltered. "Is this a bad time?"

A tall, pale-skinned Sollirian male with towering crystal horns and white waves of hair falling to his strong jawline paused awkwardly before the bed. Inez peered at him over her shoulder, her hair pasted to her face with sweat. His breeches clung to all the right places and his shirt was loose, the top button undone to reveal the peaks of a muscular chest. If Inez's nipples weren't already painfully hard, they would be at the sight of him.

Calanthe let out a long sigh. "I guess not. What do you want, brother?"

Her mistress had never mentioned a brother. Sollir wasn't dynastic and each new leader had to fight their way to the title. Calanthe had staged her coup by seducing the last emperor, stabbing him to death on their wedding night, and dropping half the imperial court on Janus to die. While her birth family didn't matter, surely someone would have mentioned—

"Stepbrother," Rylec corrected.

Calanthe sighed. She handed the whip to a servant and patted Inez twice on the shoulder. "You can come now."

The wave of pleasure was immediate. It rippled through Inez's thoughts, her body. Her back arched, her mouth opening in one loud groan. She clutched at the footboard and tried to hold it in, but Calanthe desired her embarrassment above all else. Inez wanted to close her eyes and pretend she was alone, but her traitorous gaze caught on the male. Calanthe's stepbrother. But he didn't watch her shiver and scream and bleed with scorn or a wicked desire. He stared at her blankly, his dark eyes containing something almost like... fury. And when his gaze flickered to Calanthe, that fury morphed and grew, mixed with disgust.

Both emotions were gone in a flash, like Inez had dreamed it.

Real or not, Calanthe didn't notice it as she meandered to the room's elaborate bar cart, poured two drinks, and raised one toward her stepbrother. "Talk, Rylec."

Rylec's eyes traced back to Inez, naked and slumped against the footboard. The orgasm had finally finished with her, but her rough pants echoed throughout the room. Inez wanted to crawl away and cry. But until her mistress said she could go, she lay still in her own drying blood.

Rylec raised his hand and the drink in Calanthe's floated over to him. Telekinetic, then. "In front of your star-maid?"

"She's not going to talk." Calanthe dropped lazily into a chair. "She's far too scared of me to do that."

Inez's heart shriveled. Of course Calanthe knew. Sometimes the empress pretended they were friends, lovers, or a lady and her favorite maid. Inez had learned to smile and laugh at her jokes, to blush at her confessions of affection, and to gossip about the fawning idiots of the imperial court. But at the end of the day, Inez was simply Calanthe's star-maid and property, to do with as she wished.

Inez glanced at the ceiling, not wanting to see her mistress's smirk or her stepbrother's reaction, but she didn't look away quick enough. This time, the fury was clear as day on Rylec's face.

Calanthe scoffed. "Don't look at me that way, brother. She's a star-maid. Her soul and her body are mine to use as I please."

Hot tea swished out of the cup, burning Inez's hand and the memory. Dammit. Inez swallowed the pain. She had tried so hard to forget her time with Calanthe. Hours and hours of therapy had helped, but nothing could ever erase the memories of what she had suffered. Inez had been whipped for the first time at age ten, but no amount of preparation readied her for Calanthe's cruel blend of pain and pleasure. Every other Sollirian she had encountered picked one and stuck with it.

Inez looked Calanthe straight in the eye. "I remember. I remember everything."

Calanthe smiled, a strange wistfulness. "Good. I'm glad."

Empress Calanthe lifted a tiny silver bell and rang it, a twinkle echoing through the room. A Sollirian nursemaid rushed in and bowed. Soriya started to pout, but Calanthe reached out and brushed a hand down the girl's dark curls. "Mama has to speak to her guests about serious adult matters, Soriya. Go with your nursemaid, please."

Soriya reluctantly lowered her cup. "Yes, Mama."

"Good girl." Calanthe ruffled her hair. "Mama loves you."

"I love you, too, Mama."

The little girl toddled from the room, followed by the obedient maid. Inez watched her go, enraptured by every step. Across the table, Rylec did the same. When the doors shut, her eyes met his. They burned with a fury greater than she had ever seen. Getting their daughter back was more important than ever.

Rylec lowered his cup and leaned back in his chair, all pretense of civility gone. "What do you want, Calanthe?"

"Can't I have tea with my stepbrother and his wife and not want anything else but their company?"

"No." Inez lowered her teacup, too. She hadn't drunk a sip of the liquid and there was no reason to pretend for her daughter's sake any longer. "What do you want, Calanthe?"

Calanthe's gaze widened. "Oh, my. Rylec, what did you do to my little dove? She was so tiny and meek when I gifted her to you."

"I didn't do anything to her, Calanthe. I let her be herself."

Inez's heart panged. He truly had let her be herself. Rylec had never demanded or chastised or threatened. He had let her be and let her grow. That was why she had fallen in love with him. It was why she loved him still. Her heart nearly burst. She had stomped down on her emotions for so long. It was the only way to survive the separation. But now, Inez let herself feel everything.

"Egh, boring." Calanthe reached across the table, her hands like a striking snake. She gripped both Inez and Rylec. Inez recoiled, but her disgust melted away in a second, replaced by a burning fire of desire in her core. By the way Rylec stiffened, he felt it too. "Where's the passion? Where's the heat? You two are married, for the gods' sake."

"No offense," Rylec gritted out, "but your presence entirely ruins the mood."

The burning desire whipped into an inferno. Inez bit her lip to swallow a groan. Calanthe grinned and purred. "Does it now?"

Inez dug her nails into her skin, trying to cut through the sensation. "Let go, Calanthe."

"Or what, little dove? You're my prisoners. With Rylec cuffed, he can't stop me. You never could. I can do whatever I want to do."

"And what do you want?" Rylec gritted out.

"Oh, quite simple." Calanthe pulled back suddenly, cutting off her connection. Inez slumped in relief, the desperation in her core fading. Across the table, Rylec didn't react, but relief sparked in his eyes.

And then Calanthe opened her terrible mouth. "I want you two to make me another baby."

CHAPTER 11

His stepsister had finally lost what little sanity she had left.

Inez clearly agreed. Her jaw had dropped upon Calanthe's announcement, but she managed to snap it shut. "Excuse me?"

"You heard me, little dove. I want another baby. Soriya is the perfect daughter, and it's about time I have another." Calanthe leaned toward Inez and whispered conspiratorially, "I promised her a sister, you know. Keep that in mind."

Rylec had no words. His star-wife looked at him with a wild panic in her eyes. Rage flared to life within him. If Rylec weren't cuffed, he'd snap Calanthe's neck with a single thought for the things she had said and done to his mate. But Rylec couldn't access anything more than a wisp of his magic. "You've lost your mind, Calanthe."

Calanthe leaned back and rolled her eyes. "So they say."

Inez pushed from her seat. "I'm not—we're not—"

"You're not what? Pregnant? I know. I hoped. That would have made this much easier, but I guess not even you can impregnate a female in one day, brother."

Rylec twitched. There was a time he considered Calanthe his sister. Their parents had married when he was young. Calanthe's mother had as much interest in her daughter as Emperor Oriel did his son. But time and experience had made her cruel. He didn't begrudge her when she seduced his father and took the crown. That was the Sollirian way. But what she had done after, to Inez and so many others, was inexcusable. In his mind, his sister died the moment she first sat on the throne. "I'm not your brother, Calanthe."

Calanthe went still and silent, her kaleidoscope eyes focused on him. Rylec didn't back down from the glare. In some ways, the empress was like a wild animal. Turning your back on her only resulted in an attack.

After a long moment, Calanthe shuddered, coming out of whatever madness gripped her and picked up that infuriating little bell. With a ring, a Sollirian in the red of a doctor entered, pushing a cart of tools and gadgets. "This is my personal physician, Doctor Camden. What do you have for us today, Doctor?"

"The pills you requested, Your Majesty." Doctor Camden plucked a tiny bottle filled with green pills from his cart. "Nanite-based pills to ensure conception."

Rylec clenched his fists. Nanite pills? Calanthe was desperate.

Inez pushed back her seat. "No, I'm not—"

Calanthe grabbed Inez's hand. His wife went down with an agonizing cry. Rylec launched from his seat with a snarl. His magic strained at his cuff, but though he could feel the power, it was out of reach. Calanthe's guard rushed forward, but Rylec's elbow shot back, catching the male in the chest. Nothing would keep him from his mate.

Calanthe spun, putting Inez before her like a shield. "Come any closer, Rylec, and I'll kill her instantly."

Rylec froze.

"Good boy." Her grip tightened on Inez's wrist. "As for you, little dove, you will take your pill. Rylec will take his. You'll go over to that bed and as my brother fucks you, you'll think of all that time we spent together under those sheets. Once he's finished, Doctor Camden here will perform his tests. When he confirms you're pregnant, you and I will return to Sollir to prepare for our new baby. Together."

Rylec growled, but the sound was lost under Inez's shout. "There's no way, you psycho—"

His mate's voice cut off into a scream as Calanthe upped the pain. "If you don't, I'll kill Rylec."

Inez stopped struggling. Those perfect green eyes found his. Gods, he was failing her again. The guard stood behind him and Calanthe still had her hands on his mate, so Rylec focused all his attention on his cuffs. As an archlord with a star-wife, he should be able to access his magic with great strain. He didn't care if he hurt himself. Not if Inez was in trouble.

For now, he would take Calanthe's wrath. "And how will you get me to comply, *sister*?"

Calanthe released Inez's wrist. His mate dropped, her face flushed and her breathing wild, as the empress circled the table. "Inez will leave this room pregnant, no matter what, Rylec. If you don't do it, I'll find a volunteer." She placed a delicate hand on his shoulder. "And before I kill you, I'll make you watch."

Rylec slammed forward with a roar. That bitch—

Pain radiated through his nervous system. Rylec almost dropped to his knees, but he kept his balance. He had endured worse.

It lasted only a moment before Calanthe lowered her hand and walked around him, putting her guard between them. Her fingers trailed over a gilded wristlet that flashed the time into the air. "You have an hour."

With that, the empress strolled from the room, humming as she walked. The doors slammed shut behind her and locked.

Rylec rushed around the table, desperate for Inez's touch. His wife moved, too, and nearly threw herself in his arms. Rylec wrapped her in his embrace. Gods, he never wanted to see her in pain again. They shouldn't have done this. They should have run. A part of him knew that if they had they'd never have seen Soriya again, but he hated seeing her in pain.

Inez pressed her cheek against his chest. "How close are you to escaping that cuff?"

"I won't have them off in an hour."

She inhaled deeply. "I don't want to give her another baby. She stole Soriya. Our little girl thinks that monster is her mother."

He brushed a hand down her thick hair. "We'll get her back, Inez."

"But to get her back, we have to live." Inez pulled back to look at him. "There's no choice. If we both want to live, I need to be pregnant in an hour. If we do what Calanthe wants, I'm sure she'll order her guard away. I'll be alone with her and then I can strike."

His star-wife had already made too many sacrifices in her life. He couldn't let her make another. "We'll find another way."

"There's no other way."

"Inez—"

She pulled out of his arms and returned to the table. The doctor had left behind the two small pills. Inez swallowed one without a second thought. She tossed the other at him before removing her cloak. "Take off your clothes, Rylec."

For a moment, Rylec didn't move, but one look into her eyes melted his resolve. This was what his wife wanted. For her, he would do anything.

He swallowed the pill.

Rylec tugged his shirt over his head, his gaze on his mate. Her eyes watered. Rylec reached for his pants—

Inez grabbed his wrist. "No. Never mind. You're right. If we don't want to do this, then we won't do it."

He placed his other hand over hers on his wrist. Inez was right. It was their only way out. In an hour, he'd be closer to breaking out of his cuff. In two or three, he'd be free with his magic returned to him. He could help her in her fight against Calanthe. If this needed to happen for them to survive the next three hours and save their family, Rylec would do it. "I want this. I want you. I've always wanted you."

"Rylec, I—"

Rylec drifted his hand up her arm to the crook of her neck. He tilted her head as he leaned down to claim her pink lips. The taste of her exploded on his tongue. Inez sunk into his arms. He pulled her closer until her warm body molded against his perfectly.

They fit together like two pieces of a puzzle. He wouldn't let anything tear them apart.

Rylec wrapped his hands around her waist and plucked her from the ground.

Inez moaned into his mouth. "Not the bed."

"Tell me where and I'll do it. I'll do anything for you."

Inez caressed a hand across his face and up the length of one horn. "The bathroom."

Of course. She had told him how the bathroom was the one safe space she had from Calanthe. His stepsister always loathed getting wet. Her mother had had an infatuation with drowning people.

Rylec crossed the room and kicked open the bathroom door.

"Fill the tub," he said to the room's systems. Water quickly sputtered from the gilded tap.

Rylec lowered his wife to the countertop. He kissed down her neck, his hands slipping down her body. With a flick of a few buttons, her dress was loose and gaping. He nipped at her collarbone. Her grip tightened on his horns. Rylec resisted a groan.

Suddenly, Rylec was pushed back as his star-wife stood. In one smooth motion, her dress slipped down and pooled at her feet. She wasn't wearing any underwear. Rylec wanted to be angry at whoever dressed her, but he didn't care. His eyes devoured the valley of her curves. His cock hardened to a rod.

"You're wearing too much clothes." Inez waved her hands. The buttons of his shirt popped, and the fabric slid from his shoulders.

Rylec couldn't resist a smirk. "And you judged me for using my magic on you."

"That was different."

"How?"

She stopped an inch away from him, perfect and beautiful, with her plush breasts and her smooth stomach and the curve of her ass. His mate. His wife.

His forever.

Inez spun her hand. His trousers loosened. They didn't tumble to the floor like her outfit, but his wife didn't plan on waiting for gravity. With another flick of her fingers, they fell to the ground. Her eyes dropped to the thick length of his cock.

She licked her lips.

Rylec almost exploded on her right there.

The bathroom dinged as the tub finished filling behind them. Inez didn't break her gaze from his throbbing length. "Get in the tub, Rylec."

Rylec didn't argue. He didn't want to. Without taking his eyes from her beautiful body, he backed up and stepped into the tub. The warm water lapped against his skin. His nerve endings were on fire with anticipation. He lowered himself into the water and stretched back, his abs rippling.

Inez's eyes followed the movement. It lured her forward. When she stepped into the tub, his entire body tensed. He had waited for this day for three years.

Rylec couldn't wait anymore.

He slid his hands up her thighs to the curve of her ass and pulled her to him. She didn't resist. If anything, she threw herself

forward. Their lips crashed together. Raven-
ous for each other.

He needed her now.

Rylec spread her legs until she straddled
his thighs and pulled her down. He plunged
into her warm heat. Inez jerked, breaking the
kiss to let out a deep moan.

He wanted to pulse into her, claim her, but
instead he said, "If you want me to stop, all
you have to do is say the words."

Her body shuddered. "Don't stop."

Rylec obeyed her command. He settled his
hands on her waist and thrust himself into
her body again and again. She gripped his
horns, her back arching. Her breasts bounced
with the movement. Her green eyes shone
wild with passionate. Gods, she was the most
beautiful thing he had ever seen.

"More, Rylec, more," she shouted.

Rylec pulled out of her and spun her body
around. Her hands gripped the tub's rim.
He spread the plump curves of her ass and
pulsed into her hot center again. He slipped
in deep. He groaned, the sound almost near a

roar. Rylec wanted to stay inside her forever with their bodies intertwined.

"Faster," Inez moaned.

Rylec's thrusts grew wild. Inez pushed back, matching every movement. The pressure in Rylec swelled and burned and grew.

But he couldn't come, not yet. Not without her. He traced a hand around her thigh and brushed a knuckle against her clit. Inez jerked at the touch. Water splashed from the tub.

"I'm going..." Inez panted. "I think I'm going..."

Inez screamed out his name as her body clenched around his. Milking his cock. Rylec exploded in a rush of heat. Gods, he loved her. Loved her more than anything in this universe. His hips thrust up wildly, staking their claim. Inez was his. Soriya was his. The child they made right now was his.

He wouldn't let Calanthe have any of them.

CHAPTER 12

I nez eyed Doctor Camden as he waved the scanner down her body. The guards had escorted Rylec away once their hour was up, leaving her alone with Calanthe and the doctor. Inez shuffled uncomfortably in her seat at the end of the bed. The doctor probably didn't have magic. Anyone with powerful abilities became a lord, and those with weaker gifts worked in security. If anything, he might be able to heal.

Still, Inez waited. The Sollirians didn't cuff her because they didn't think she could use Rylec's magic. Her training was short, but it would be enough if she got Calanthe alone. The empress would *never* have her again.

Doctor Camden stopped his waving and tapped on the thin tablet before him.

Calanthe stopped her pacing. "So?"

"The nanites were successful. The star-maid is pregnant."

Inez touched her belly as Calanthe *squee*-ed. A rush of emotions rose within her, shock and surprise and anger and delight. They passed through her so fast she could barely process them. She and Rylec were having another baby. When Soriya had quickened within her, Inez had loved every minute of it. This time, if she couldn't subdue the empress, her pregnancy would be a prison.

Inez couldn't fail.

A sharp ringing ripped through her concentration. Calanthe rang her little bell with the enthusiasm of a young child. When a servant ran in, she snapped, "Bring Soriya."

Damn. Inez couldn't make a move in front of Soriya. Her daughter didn't know her. If Inez killed Calanthe, Soriya would never see her as a mother.

Calanthe swirled back around, her dress a twirl of soft fabric. "Aren't you excited, Inez?"

Inez forced a smile. "I am."

The empress's smirk bared tiny fangs. "Don't lie to me, little dove."

Inez met those kaleidoscope eyes dead-on. "I'm not."

The door clicked open, summoning Calanthe's attention. Thank the Gods. Inez had become an excellent liar in the past three years, but the empress had a way of getting people to tell her the truth.

Namely, causing them extreme amounts of pain.

The nursemaid led Soriya in.

Inez's heart leapt at the sight of her daughter, but she stayed seated. Even after they got rid of Calanthe, it would take time for her daughter to get comfortable with her and Rylec. Inez would give her all the space she needed.

Calanthe crouched before the small child. "I have good news, baby dove. You're going to have a sibling soon."

"Mama is having a baby?" Soriya reached out, wrapping her arms around Calanthe's neck. Inez stiffened. If Calanthe wanted, she could cause her daughter unimaginable pain. When the empress walked toward her with Soriya in her grip, the look in her eyes was almost gleeful.

"Yes, Mama is having a baby. With Auntie Inez's help. She will carry your brother or sister like she carried you."

Soriya glanced down at Inez. Was this the first time her daughter had looked at her? Truly looked at her? Perhaps. Inez sat straight and stiff. She would *not* react. Calanthe wouldn't get that pleasure.

Calanthe crouched and reached out, placing a hand on Inez's stomach. Nausea swirled in her gut. "Want to touch, Soriya? Your new sibling is right here."

"Wow." A tiny hand settled over Inez's belly. The softness of her touch chased away the fear from Calanthe's. Inez wanted to caress a hand down her daughter's face, ruffle the loose, dark curls they both shared. But Calanthe needed to think Inez had resigned herself to obedience if she had a chance of being alone with the empress.

Inez memorized every inch of her daughter's face, but the hair on her neck prickled. A predator watched them both, waiting to pounce.

After an eternal moment, Calanthe stood and handed Soriya back to the nursemaid. "Mama and Auntie Inez need to have a chat now, baby dove."

"But Mama..."

"The three of us can have tea when we return to Sollir this afternoon."

Inez's heart stuttered. *This* afternoon. She shouldn't be surprised. Calanthe had what she wanted. Why stay any longer? The female always hated visiting Tertia. It was why she sent Rylec to govern the planet after all. The empress couldn't send him any further from the throne without banishing him outright.

The trap around Inez was closer. She needed to act. Now.

Soriya waved as the nursemaid left the room, followed by the doctor. Inez didn't glance at Calanthe's guard. She didn't want to be too obvious.

Calanthe stared back, assessing Inez. After a long moment, she pointed at her guard. "Out."

The male didn't question the order. He nodded obediently, dropped into a bow, and marched from the room.

The click of the door echoed like the shot of a gun through the now-empty chambers. Inez did her best not to jump. This was her chance. *Her* only chance.

Calanthe approached with the lazy prowl of a predator. Was the empress expecting a fight? Possibly. Inez hadn't held her tongue during tea. But Calanthe didn't understand what she was capable of—as a person or as a mother.

"If I could change my magic, I'd be a mind reader," she said. "What are you thinking, little dove?"

Inez could've spun a lie from nothing, but she didn't want to lie anymore. She stayed seated, waiting, watching, and told a truth. "I'm worried."

Calanthe leaned against the post at the end of the bed. "Do not fret, little dove. You are with child again. I wasn't there when you were pregnant with Soriya, but the spies I had on my brother reported she brought you much joy. Once you birth our second child and hold them in your arms, you'll be happy again."

"My second child."

Calanthe's kaleidoscope eyes narrowed. "Pardon?"

Inez kept her chin high. "My second child. This baby is mine and Rylec's, just like Soriya. Not yours."

The empress slid closer, within reach. Inez braced for the pain. Let Calanthe think she only had words as weapons. Agony zapped through her skin like a stab of hot iron. Inez bit down on her lip, holding in the scream—

Calanthe leaned away, breaking the connection. Inez slumped onto the cushion. "No. I won't harm our baby. She's too new. The pain may cause you to miscarry. I can't have that."

Inez managed a snort. "You can just summon Rylec to fuck me again, so why does it matter?"

A strange light entered Calanthe's eyes. She leaned forward suddenly and cupped Inez's cheek with a coo. "Oh, my dear Inez. I am powerful, but not even I can bring back the dead."

Everything within Inez stopped. *Not even she could bring back the dead...* Her brain refused to process it.

Until it suddenly did. The world narrowed to Calanthe before her. "Excuse me?"

"I ordered Archlord Eliaz to execute Rylec. He's committed high crimes against me one too many times. He's my stepbrother, yes, but I can't spare him again. What will my archlords think of me?" Calanthe's hand trailed from Inez's chin to neck, tracing lower, but she didn't feel it. Didn't see it. Her vision pulsed, not with fear, but with rage. "And therefore, I can't hurt you, Inez. But I can punish you in other ways…"

Calanthe reached the end of Inez's skirts and reached into the folds, her magic infecting her skin. Her nipples hardened. Inez dug her nails into her palm. No. Not again. *Never* again. Inez grabbed hold of that invading lust and twisted it. Desire was a primal urge, a shock of energy through the system, a flash of heat. If pain was the cousin to fear, then lust was the brother to anger.

Inez lashed out with a scream of rage. Her knee collided with Calanthe's face before her foot shoved the empress off her.

The empress crashed to the floor. Inez didn't wait for her to make her next move. She rolled across the bed and landed on her feet. If Calanthe yelled out and her guard entered, Inez would be in trouble. She couldn't let this chance pass her by.

Inez focused on Rylec's magic and pulled—

Calanthe jumped to her feet and spun out of the way.

Goddammit.

Calanthe spit out a glob of blood onto her once-stainless gold floors. "Now, now, little dove. I don't want to hurt you."

Seriously? Even after attacking her, Calanthe still didn't believe she was a threat.

Calanthe took her silence as submission. "I plan to make you my star-wife. Once Rylec is dead, your tether will be broken. You will be tethered to me again and this time, I will tether myself to you. You'll be Empress Consort of Sollir, the first star-maid to ever claim the title. We will raise our daughters—"

Inez didn't want to hear a minute more of this nightmare. "My daughters, you evil bitch."

Calanthe's eyes went hard—

Inez pulled on Rylec's magic and slammed out, focusing it on the empress. It blasted through the room like a tidal wave. Powered by her anger and her fear and her love. She would reclaim Soriya. She would save Rylec.

Inez would never be weak again. She would never again be Calanthe's pet.

The bed and the chairs skid across the floor. Calanthe flew across the room and whacked into the wall, her head snapping back. She dropped to the floor in a mass of pale skirts.

A slow and steady pool of red stained the white.

Empress Calanthe didn't move again.

CHAPTER 13

R ylec paced the small cell, his fists clenched at his side. He went reluctantly when the empress's guards came for him after his and Inez's hour was up. Inez hadn't smiled or nodded as they escorted him out, but he saw the determination in her eyes. Calanthe would slip up. She never saw his star-wife as a threat—only as a possession. She had pawned her off to Rylec when she was bored, only to try to claim her back after Soriya's birth.

But still. Rylec was a Sollirian male. It was his duty to protect his wife and child.

Children.

Rylec pressed his back to the cell's icy wall and closed his eyes. His magic was distant with the cuff on his wrist, but he sensed it there within him, a swaying sea of energy. A normal lord wouldn't be able to access his magic, but archlords were archlords for a reason. And Rylec was more than an archlord. He was an archlord with a star-wife, her life-force boosting his magic with just her presence.

He weaved his magic through the cuff, examining their mechanism. Since the guards placed them on him hours ago, he had already tweaked and prodded them closer to opening. With a few more minutes—

His cage clanged open.

Rylec didn't move, but he opened his eyes with a glare at the ready. One of the empress's guards pushed open the door, but it was Archlord Eliaz who entered.

Rylec didn't bother to avert his eyes. He knew how to hide from the Tertian lord.

The blue-eyed male smiled brightly. "Rylec. I hear congratulations are in order. Star-maid Inez is pregnant."

A wave of possessiveness swept through Rylec. Inez, pregnant with his child. The first time it had happened, he had hidden his star-wife away from the public, hoping to slow the spread of news to Calanthe. This time, he couldn't protect her by taking her away. His enemies were circling and needed to be dealt with once and for all.

"Is that all you're here for, Eliaz?"

"No, of course not. You're being moved."

"Ah." Rylec didn't say any more. He didn't need to. By moved, Eliaz meant killed. The empress had promised Rylec his life if they did what she wanted, but Rylec had always doubted it. Calanthe wasn't ever to be trusted.

But it had bought them time, and that was all that mattered. Rylec gestured for Eliaz to lead the way. Once the male turned around, Rylec returned his focus to the cuff on his wrist. He just needed a few more minutes.

The Imperial Guards slammed the cell's door shut behind him before taking position at the rear. Eliaz strolled ahead, hands linked behind his back. The guards pushed Rylec forward, but they couldn't challenge Eliaz's pace. Without their empress's presence, Archlord Eliaz was the highest-ranked Sollirian here.

"Where am I being moved to?" Rylec didn't want to start a conversation, but if he didn't at least ask, the archlord might wonder what else was preoccupying his mind.

"A more... permanent cell."

Otherwise known as death. The archlord was usually more subtle than this. But Eliaz hated Calanthe. Most of the lords on Tertia did, which was why they were assigned territory as far as possible from her. Inez had asked him who his contact was on the Tertian council. Was it Eliaz? The male loved risks, but this seemed extreme, even for him. If he helped Rylec and failed, Eliaz would be put to death beside him.

Rylec would ask once he had the upper hand.

Which he would in three... two... one.

His cuff clicked open.

The sound was soft, but in the silent hallway, it echoed like the shot of a cannon. One of the Imperial Guards grabbed his shoulder—

Rylec placed a hand over the male's. "Thanks."

He speared his magic through their connection, shattering and snapping every bone he came in contact with. The guard's arm went limp as he screamed, but the sound cut off when Rylec reached the spine. With one tug, he snapped the vertebrae.

The guard slumped to the floor, dead.

Rylec turned on the other. The guard had summoned the tiniest ball of fire. He snorted. Pathetic. He focused his magic on the male's hand and like a child with a doll, forced the guard's hand to slap into his own face.

The hand with the fire, of course.

The guard shrieked and flailed as he burned. Rylec didn't wait for him to die. Neither of the guards were the biggest threat in the room. While he turned, Rylec sensed something at his back. He pushed out with all his might—

Eliaz slammed into the wall, pinned to the stone by the force of Rylec's magic.

Rylec didn't look away in time.

Those bright blue eyes lasered into his, growing brighter and brighter—

Rylec flinched away from the light. When he turned back around, he was no longer in the halls of the Tertian palace, but in a quaint solarium, scattered with seating areas, cushions, and the odd child's toy.

What the fuck.

"Rylec."

Rylec spun. Eliaz now sat in a chair by the window, overlooking burgundy fields. The archlord considered him. "The empress didn't order you to a new cell."

"I'm not an idiot, Eliaz." Rylec reached for his magic. It was still there, but as long as he was in Eliaz's mind, he couldn't use it on anything. Rylec imagined a protective bubble around his skin. It wouldn't help if Eliaz attempted anything in here, but if the male tried to kill him in the real world, his magic would deflect the attack. "She ordered my death."

"I have a proposition for you."

Obviously. "I'm listening."

"I want Tertia. Entirely. The rest of the empire can burn for all I care, since we won't be a part of it. When our planet joined with Sollir, it was a beacon, a force that couldn't be reckoned with. Over the last century, the Sollir Empire has become more and more disjointed. Mismanaged by a dozen empresses and emperors, your own father included."

Rylec crossed the fake-room and dropped into the opposite chair. "If you think that will insult me, you don't know me as well as you claim, Eliaz."

"I didn't mean it as an insult." With a wave of the male's hands, drinks appeared at their side table. Rylec plucked up his cup and took a sip. Decent for a non-existent drink. "I was there when you were sent word of Emperor Oriel's death and Empress Calanthe's crowning. You reacted more to the news of your stepsister-turned-stepmother."

"Calanthe was always a brute."

"She was." Eliaz sipped at his own drink for dramatic pause. Everything was a show to the male. "Which is why I want to get out from under her unholy thumb."

Rylec lowered the drink. "You're my contact."

"I am."

Rylec didn't repress his snort. Eliaz had always been a possibility, but Rylec would have put credits down on Naccius or Severin. Those males loved their secrets. But Archlord Eliaz, ruler of Tertia? He was basically a king. "Why?"

"Why do you think, Rylec? You know me. The son of a lowly archlord and one of her many star-maids, banished to Lucien Manor because they already had half a dozen young lords to train." Eliaz leaned forward and rested an elbow on his crossed legs. "You trained because your father wanted more for you. I trained because I wanted to prove my mother wrong. I was the lord they should've kept. By the time she realized, I was already beyond her. Tertia is mine now. I have more than a small territory, I have a planet. I won't let anyone take it from me."

Ah. The obvious answer, then. If Rylec had known Eliaz was itching for rebellion, maybe the two of them could have joined forces years ago. "So what do you propose?"

"I let you go. You kill Calanthe."

"You want me to claim the Imperial Throne?"

"At least temporarily. As long as you grant Tertia her independence, you can run off with your star-wife after for all I care."

Eliaz stirred his drink, but Rylec wasn't fooled by the casual motion. If he said no, then he was Eliaz's enemy. The male would treat him in kind. But would he say no? His priority was to save Inez and Soriya. On Tertia, Eliaz was the best partner to have.

"Deal."

The room faded to black instantly, the window and chairs and drinks disappearing. All that remained was glowing blue eyes. He had given Eliaz exactly what he wanted.

But Rylec would get what he wanted too.

In the space of a blink, Rylec returned to his body standing in the hall. Eliaz had dusted himself off the wall but hadn't approached. Startling an archlord was never a healthy decision.

Rylec stepped over the dead guards, back in the direction of his mate. "I'm getting my wife."

Eliaz sighed. "Don't be reckless, Rylec. You're making me regret my life choices already."

"I'm not leaving her with Calanthe."

"How about we make a plan—"

Two guards wearing the imperial crest rounded the corner.

Everyone froze. Rylec and Eliaz eyed the guards. The guards eyed the bodies. Rylec and Eliaz eyed the bodies. The guards eyed Rylec and Eliaz. After five seconds of intense staring, the guards pulled their swords in an arch of electrified silver.

But they didn't charge straight away. Id-iots. One yelled out, "Archlord Eliaz, is there a problem?"

Eliaz hooked a thumb into his pockets. "No, not at all."

"You—" the guard choked on the rest of his sentence.

Eliaz sighed rather dramatically. Both guards were caught in the web of those bright eyes. "Unfortunately, I won't be bring-ing Rylec to the square for execution. Not today at least."

Both guards spun around with their swords out. Their blades cut into each oth-er with a wet splat, pulsing multi-colored blood out onto the palace's floors. With a few twitches, the guards tumbled to the ground, joining their comrades in death.

Eliaz sighed again. "I just had these floors polished."

"If we don't save my wife, that will be the least of your concerns."

"Was that a threat, Rylec?"

Before Rylec replied, two more guards rounded the corner. Gods have mercy. Rylec flung out a hand and pasted them to the far wall. Better to be safe.

But no imperial crest lined the sleek uniforms.

"Those are mine," Eliaz said.

"Are you sure?"

Eliaz glanced into both their eyes. "Yes."

Rylec dropped them.

Eliaz gestured to the hallway's multiple bleeding corpses. "Clean up the mess, will you? Lord Rylec and I have business to attend to."

One of the guards nervously licked her lips. "My lord, we come with news. It's the empress. We think... we think she's dead."

CHAPTER 14

Inez stared at Calanthe's body for a thousand years.

In reality, it wasn't more than a minute. But her brain couldn't process the sight in front of her. Calanthe, still and solid, the blood pouring from her head wound slowing to a trickle.

Inez had meant to kill her, but she had always imagined the monster's death as more dramatic.

Then her personal guard charged into the room.

Fuck.

Inez didn't know what type of magic the guard had, only that he would be far weaker than Rylec.

A dagger flew toward her head.

Inez dodged. Where had that even come from?

The guard waved his hand and another dagger appeared.

Ah. From there.

Inez had trained in hand-to-hand combat for years, but never with anyone who could summon a new weapon mid-fight. Then again, last time she fought, she hadn't had magic of her own. She raised her hand and the dagger impaled in the bed post flew into her grip. With a flick of her wrist, Inez threw the blade. The guard tried to dodge, but Inez hadn't thrown the blade with her hand, but with magic. She tracked his movement with her eyes and the blade followed.

It caught him in the neck, and he crashed to the floor with a gurgled crash.

"Phew," she huffed out, but Inez didn't let herself relax. Calanthe surely had more guards. An entire fleet had arrested her and Rylec.

Rylec.

Inez ran from the room. She didn't care who she encountered on the other side. Rylec wouldn't go to his death easily, but wherever he was, he needed help. Inez had fled last time, letting a cruise ship carry her to the other side of the galaxy. She wouldn't leave him alone again.

Inez crashed into a solid male body as she swung out the door.

She bounced off and landed softly on her feet.

Archlord Eliaz raised a dark eyebrow. "Inez."

Inez redirected her eyes. She couldn't take her attention off Eliaz, so she stared at the side of his head. Rylec had once said the archlord needed direct eye contact to read and control a mind.

"Where's Rylec?"

"Where's Calanthe?"

"Dead." If the archlord gave her the same answer in return, she'd kill him.

But Rylec couldn't be dead. His magic still thrummed under her skin. As long as they were both on Tertia, she would know.

"Not dead."

Bastard. With magic, Inez pulled the dagger from the guard's neck on the other side of the room. When the blade landed in her grip, she raised it at him. "Where is he?"

For some reason, the psychopath grinned. "How did Calanthe die?"

What? Her furrowed brow conveyed the question, but Eliaz's eyebrow just arched higher.

Fine. Whatever. What did it matter? "I killed her."

"Ah. In that case, Rylec is right this way, Your Majesty." Eliaz dropped into a bow—

not a very low one, but noticeably a bow.

Inez stared. Her Majesty? "What are you doing?"

Before the archlord answered, Rylec spun around the corner. Blood splattered his once-white shirt and pale skin, but it didn't look like his. The shade was too orange, drying to a burnt color on his white skin. Inez lowered the blade, but didn't take her eyes off of Eliaz.

"Next time you decide to transport yourself, Eliaz," her husband started, "bring me along with you—Inez?"

Inez dropped the blade and ran for him. Eliaz shuffled out of the way. If he hadn't, Inez would have run him down. Nothing could keep her away from her mate. Her living, breathing star-husband. Rylec opened his arms and Inez crashed into them. Home. It wasn't a place or a nation, but a single person. Him. It always had been.

"Are you hurt?" he asked, the words a whisper in her ear.

"I'm okay." Her mind remembered the pain Calanthe had caused her, but her body had already forgotten. And the monster was dead. She could sleep soundly at night for the first time in years. "And you?"

"I'm fine." Rylec pulled back, just enough to look over her shoulder. "What happened?"

Inez wasn't sure if he was asking Eliaz or her, but she answered before the archlord. "I killed Calanthe."

Rylec processed the words in a single blink. "She's finally dead."

Inez nodded. "Finally."

This time, her husband's gaze clearly went to Eliaz. "And did Eliaz help?"

"I arrived after, I'm afraid."

Inez glanced between the two males. "Why?"

"We made an agreement." Rylec narrowed his eyes at the Tertian archlord. "One that is now void."

"Is it, though?" Eliaz leaned against the wall and crossed his arms, an infuriatingly casual pose. "You're in my palace on my planet. Do you have any loyal guards nearby to protect all you hold dear?"

"Don't threaten us, Eliaz," Inez snapped. She was so tired of archlords telling her what to do.

"Already so much like an empress."

An empress? He had called her by the imperial title before but thought him deranged. "What are you talking about?"

"You know how our society works. Whoever kills the current leader becomes the new leader."

"That rule only applies to Sollirians." That piece of information had been drilled into Inez since she started her star-maid training. If the law had applied to everyone, star-maids would try to kill the empress daily.

Eliaz strolled closer, closing the distance between them. "You're a star-*wife*, Inez. Through our laws, that technically makes you a Sollirian citizen. As long as Rylec lives, you share rights and titles. Calanthe refused to acknowledge your relationship, but it doesn't make it any less true."

Inez looked back to Rylec, but her mate didn't counter his point. If anything, his jaw clenched tighter. Rylec had spent a decade of his life as the child of an imperial emperor. He knew the dangers imperial life brought. "What is he saying?"

Rylec met her gaze. "You're the Empress of Sollir."

Inez stared. That couldn't be. The Sollirians would never accept a star-maid on the throne. Calanthe had suggested it, but she was crazy. But Rylec wasn't crazy. Eliaz wasn't crazy. If they both said it was true...

Eliaz gestured at himself. "And that's why you need an ally."

Rylec shot a glare at the other male, who halted his approach. "Not now, Eliaz."

Inez opened and closed her mouth, but no sound came out. "But I can't..."

"You are." Rylec squeezed her hands. "We can still leave. No one can force you to accept the throne."

"Oh, gods." Inez rubbed a hand down her face. She had never dreamed of power. She had always imagined running as far as possible from Sollir and never returning. But if she stayed, could she change the empire? The archlords would try to kill her. They wouldn't like following a star-maid's rules. She would put herself and Rylec and their children at risk.

But thousands upon thousands of star-maids lived in the empire. She could rescue herself, but she couldn't save them all.

Unless she could.

Inez wrapped her arms around her husband. "I can't make this decision alone."

"You're never alone, Inez. I'm by your side, always."

"This is your planet, Rylec. Your people."

He caressed a hand down her cheek. "None of them matter. What do you want?"

Inez swallowed. What did she want? Artema wasn't her home. Neither was Earth. She had spent most of her life within the empire. With Rylec as her emperor, could they make it a better place?

They could try.

She would never forgive herself if she didn't try. "I think I want to stay."

Rylec nodded. "Then we stay."

Eliaz cleared his throat. Inez and Rylec shot him twin glares, but the archlord had no shame. "And our deal?"

Inez didn't even need to consult Rylec to know they'd agree. "Round up Calanthe's guards. Sollir has new rulers."

"Of course, Your Majesty."

CHAPTER 15

10 Months Later

Inez dug her hands into the silk bedsheets, her head thrown back against Rylec's chest. "Oh, Gods, Rylec."

Her star-husband didn't say anything, but his body reacted, his thrusts becoming deeper and faster. His magic held up her leg, leaving his hand free to flick and tease at her clit. Inez's body arched and thrashed uncontrollably. The heat in her climbed, ready to peak, ready to send her body over the edge.

Rylec's hand slid up and over the bulging curve of her swollen belly. His head dipped until his ragged breath was in her ear. "Come for me, wife."

His next thrust struck true. Inez exploded, her body convulsing. She grabbed for Rylec's hand and screamed out his name. She didn't care about the servants in the halls overhearing and gossiping with the court. Rylec was hers and she was his, star-wife and star-husband. Nothing would break them apart again.

A thousand years later, Inez drifted down from the clouds. "I love you so much, Rylec."

"I know, wife." Rylec kissed his way from her neck to her forehead before propping his chin on her head. "I love you more and more each day."

Inez snuggled into his side, her hand linked with her husband's above her belly. Her truly massive belly. "Soriya wasn't this late."

"Alesia does what she wants. Just like her mother."

Inez squeezed his hand. "I think that's more of a you thing."

Rylec chuckled, the sound reverberating through his chest. "Is it now?"

Inez tried to twist around, to look into those intoxicating dark eyes. But at forty weeks pregnant, she was due to pop at any minute and every movement was a struggle.

She hadn't been nearly as large with Soriya. The physician had assured her she wasn't having twins, but a part of Inez didn't believe him.

Not that anyone would dare to lie to the Empress of Sollir.

Rylec sensed what she wanted and pushed onto an elbow, the strong lines of his face coming into view. The tips of his white hair brushed her skin. He had grown it out the last few months at Inez's urging. She loved a male with long hair.

Inez cupped his cheek. "I do what I want now, but I was afraid for so long. If you hadn't let me breathe and find myself, I wouldn't be the woman I am today."

"You were always that woman." He leaned down, brushing a kiss against her lips. "And I won't let anyone take her away from either of us."

"I know." Inez had lost track of the number of assassins who had come for her since news of Calanthe's death spread across Sollir. With Rylec at her side—and her newly formed

Star Guardians, an elite team of former star-maids—none had gotten close enough to do any damage. Every attempt only pushed her forward. The Sollirians feared her and the threat she presented to their old ways. Inez fought not only for herself and her growing family, but for every star-maid who had ever been kidnapped and abused.

She would fight until her dying breath.

Which, if Rylec had any say in the matter, wouldn't be for another hundred years or so.

Inez smiled up at her husband and brushed a thumb against the sharp line of his jaw. Gods, even after all this time together, his beauty struck her. The sensation swirled in her belly—

Inez's brow creased.

Rylec noticed immediately.

"What's wrong?"

"Can you help me to the bathroom?" Inez tried to stand but it wasn't the easiest position to get into anymore.

Rylec immediately moved, sliding out of bed. His magic wrapped around Inez's limbs and carried her with him. The warm embrace tickled across her skin as he deposited her onto her feet at his side. Her husband wrapped her in his embrace, a touch Inez instinctually craved—

A warm gush of fluid trickled down her legs.

Inez straightened.

"Was that—?"

"It was," Inez said, hand going to her pregnant belly. She glanced up into her husband's intense eyes. "She's coming."

RYLEC

Thirteen hours later, Inez's screams ended and their baby's cries filled the palace infirmary. Rylec clutched his wife's hand, brushing the sweat from her face and kissing her brow.

Her eyes shined with tears. "I want to see her."

Rylec didn't let her go, but he turned toward the doctors and nurses running throughout the room. A nurse finished swaddling the crying bundle and gently passed her to Rylec. He looked down into dark eyes in a red-stained, peach face. A mop of white curls stuck to her head. Two little crystalized nubs poked out of her forehead. She was perfect and beautiful, a blend of Earthling and Sollirian.

Alesia.

As Rylec turned, Inez reached out. He placed their daughter in his wife's arms. Her tears became real, streaking down her face. "She's beautiful."

Rylec gazed at the two of them. "She is."

"She's ours."

Rylec met and held her gaze. "She always will be. No one will take her from us."

Inez pressed a kiss to their daughter's forehead. The baby cooed, reaching out with tiny hands to touch her mother's face.

Rylec looked toward the door. The servant stationed there nodded and popped outside. When the doctor had announced Inez was near delivery, Rylec had summoned Soriya and her nursemaid. Things had been rough with their daughter at the start. They had done their best to shield her from Calanthe's death but had eventually told her the truth once she warmed up to her 'uncle' and 'aunt'. She didn't yet know Inez had killed her 'mother'. She was too young for that. Once she was older and realized what Calanthe had done to her, they would tell her the whole story. With the help of a qualified therapist, of course. Inez swore by the treatment.

A few moments later, his daughter entered the room. The four-year-old rushed to the bed. "I want to see."

Inez chuckled as Rylec swept Soriya up into his arms. His daughter wrapped his legs around his torso and leaned over, trying to look at her new sister. Rylec had to grab her to stop her from falling. The girl loved to climb.

Inez reached up and ruffled her hair. "Soriya, this is Alesia. She's named after my mother, just like you're named after Rylec's mother."

"Aaah-leee-seee-a," the girl drawled out, the name fumbled thanks to her missing front tooth. The doctors had said four was early for an Earthling to lose a tooth, but perfectly acceptable for a Sollirian of Rylec's genetic composition.

Inez grinned up at her, pure happiness in her gaze. "Do you want to hold her?"

"Yes, yes, yes." Soriya went feral in his arms, trying to grab for the baby. Wrangling a four-year-old was like trying to contain a small wildcat.

"Patience, Sor," Rylec said, lowering the girl to the side of his wife's bed.

"Baby, baby, baby," she shouted.

Alesia started crying, a loud wail.

Soriya jerked back in shock before her lip quivered. She opened her mouth to let out a cry to rival the newborn.

Rylec met his wife's eyes over their crying children and smiled. *I love you,* he mouthed.
Inez mouthed it back and laughed.
Rylec resisted the urge to roar with joy.

CHAPTER 16

7 Years Later

Eliaz propped one elbow on the wide expanse of polished stone table before him and rested his chin on his fist. "I don't think so."

Rylec's holographic face stayed blank and cold, but Inez frowned for a second. The Empress of Sollir quickly washed the expression off her face but Eliaz had seen it. His own lip curved, an infuriating smile. Neither the empress nor emperor were here in the flesh, but Eliaz didn't need to read their minds to know he'd win this negotiation.

If you could call it that.

"You've given me an order, but you offer nothing in return, Empress."

"She shouldn't have to," Rylec said. "She's your empress, Eliaz—"

"We're an independent colony, are we not? That was our agreement, Rylec."

His old ally glared at him. "You still have to follow our rules."

Eliaz gave a mocking little shrug. "That's not what the word independent means."

"In every other way, you're independent," Empress Inez interjected, "but not this way. This is too important."

"Oh, I know." That was exactly why Eliaz knew he'd win this. Inez was a tact negotiator, but he knew what issues mattered to her most. Though she had spent seven years as empress and twenty as a star-maid, underneath it all she was only an Earthling. An inferior species, like so many others in the galaxy. "How many assassination attempts have you faced in your seven years on the throne? Two-hundred and twenty-eight, was it?"

"If you were responsible for any of those," Rylec started with a growl—

Eliaz raised a hand. "I wouldn't have either of you killed, Rylec. A new emperor or empress might not honor our agreement. I have no desire to bend the knee again." Eliaz laid back in his seat. "Or face execution. It's more likely to go that way, I think."

Inez banged her fist against the table. The hologram projected the sound across their solar system, but given the way Rylec flinched, it had lost some of its impact in translation. "If you do not follow my order, you won't have to worry about a new empress executing you. I'll do it myself."

"The crown has made you quite bloodthirsty, Inez."

"It's 'Your Majesty', Archlord."

Eliaz inclined his head. "Your Majesty."

Inez narrowed her eyes. "Will you do it? Or do we have a problem?"

Eliaz let out a long sigh, but flicked his fingers at the hologram before him, pulling up the required paperwork for his empress to see. "As you commanded six years ago, all Tertian star-maids were untethered and returned to their Star Temple. Since then, they've slaughtered all the priests and barricaded themselves inside. They have enough land to be self-sustaining. We have sent diplomats to negotiate, but they refuse every offer."

"This time, the offer comes from me."

"But without me, you have nothing to offer."

Inez narrowed her green eyes. They bored into him like a laser, but Eliaz had never turned away from a stare. Eye contact was all he needed to hook his power into someone's mind.

"Your magic will once again be boosted," she said.

"I've never needed a star-maid, Your Majesty. They were helpful to have around, but I wouldn't be an Archlord of Tertia if I relied on another for my power."

Inez clenched her fist. "You—"

"—need me. Make it worth my time, Empress."

Rylec took his wife's hand. "We'll find someone else."

"No one else will do it."

Rylec pointed. "He won't do it."

Eliaz propped his elbow on the table and put his chin in his hand. "On the contrary, Your Majesty, I will do anything for the right price."

"We'll give you Tertia."

"Inez—"

Eliaz ignored Rylec. The male had lost his spine to his wife a decade ago. "I'm listening."

"You will be regent of Tertia, and your first-born will inherit your ruling seat. When they come of age, Tertia will become an independent nation."

"And the Tertian Council?"

Empress Inez's frown deepened. "They will retain their seats, as your counsel. Their positions can be hereditary or elected, up to you."

"Hmm." Eliaz couldn't stop the smile from curving his lips. The things he could bribe Nassius, Kratos and Severin to do...

"In return, you will tether yourself to a star-maid, making them your star-wife. Your bride will be a willing volunteer and not forced to your side in any way. She will be your queen, not your property."

Annoying, but not an impossible task. Eliaz was rather charming. Surely, he could seduce an archlord-hating, murderous star-maid. "And if no one accepts the offer?"

"Find a way." The empress's voice held no room for compromise. She had certainly grown into her power well. "You only get your reward if you succeed. Effort doesn't matter. I've been trying for years to get a Sollirian lord or archlord to tether themselves with a willing star-maid. I outlawed slavery not tethering."

"If I may speak for my other lords, we aren't exactly keen on sharing our magic."

"Too bad."

Eliaz rapped his knuckles against the table. He would do anything to claim Tertia as his own. Eliaz hated taking orders. This agreement he had worked out with Rylec and Inez years ago had benefited him greatly, yes. He had fulfilled his part in less than a week, after delivering them safely to the throne. In the seven years since, he had ruled Tertia with little oversight. But little oversight wasn't *no* oversight.

Eliaz wanted to be free.

The decision was simple, then.

"If that's the case..." Eliaz said, drawing out his words. The empress leaned forward in her seat. "I better be on my way to the closest Star Temple."

Inez almost deflated. "You'll do it?"

"I will be tethered by the end of the day. In exchange, Tertia is mine."

Rylec and Inez glanced at each other. "Agreed."

"Kain?" His personal guard and attendant perked up from his spot by the door. "Ready my transport. We're going to the Lorician Star Temple."

"We'll send you the agreement," Rylec said.

"I'll review it on the way. I have much to do today."

Inez narrowed her eyes, but she didn't voice her concerns. They knew each other well enough by now. Eliaz would follow her rules to the letter.

Anything not spelled out was fair game.

Eliaz stood and dropped into a bow. "Your Majesties."

They both nodded before the hologram disconnected. Eliaz walked from the chamber, his grin growing broader with each step. Within the day, he'd have himself a star-wife. Within a week, she'd be with child. After the baby was born, Tertia would be his and Eliaz would be free.

And his star-wife? He'd have no need for her anymore.

The First Archlord of Tertia never lost.

Thank you for reading! Continue Archlord Eliaz's story in <u>Archlord of Lies</u>, the next

book in the *Star-Marked Mates of Sollir* series.

Not ready to say goodbye to Inez and Rylec? Join my newsletter to read a steamy bonus epilogue set directly after their meeting with Eliaz.

Want to talk about books with fellow sci-fi romance readers? Join my reader group on Facebook.

Can you do me a favor? Leaving a review on <u>Amazon</u> or <u>Goodreads</u> not only shares your enthusiasm with fellow readers but also contributes immensely to the success of *Archlord of Exile*. By doing so, you're not just supporting me, but also helping more readers discover and enjoy the series.

Sneak Peek at Book 2

For thousands of years, the Sollirians abducted children from their homeworlds to fuel their magic.

Maisie would know. She was one of them.

Twenty-seven years ago, Maisie was abducted by aliens and enslaved to be a star-maid.

Seven years ago, star-maids were freed and given land within Sollir.

Yesterday, an arrogant, gorgeous archlord named Eliaz marched up to their fortress and demanded Maisie marry him.

Well, not *her* specifically. But Maisie's not passing up the opportunity to finally escape that convent—er, fortress, and kill an archlord.

Unlike her husband-to-be, Maisie doesn't want just any

archlord. She wants her sister's killer. Maisie will marry Eliaz. She'll share his bed. She'll bear his heir. But the second she finds her target, she'll get her revenge—even if it means becoming a widow.

If only Eliaz didn't have other plans for his new star-wife...

Archlord of Lies is the second book in the *Star-Marked Mates of Sollir* series and features Archlord Eliaz meeting the spitfire that is Maisie Rapp.

Order <u>Archlord of Lies</u> now on Amazon.

Other Titles by Kate Stevens

The *Bride to an Alien Prince* Series

Kyrix

Anax

Eryx

Prax

Rivix

Set in the *Bride to an Alien Prince* Universe

Marked for the Alien Prince

Looking for a bonus scene? Visit kstevens-
books.com

About Kate Stevens

USA Today Bestselling Author Kate Stevens has been devouring romance novels and soaking up every detail since she was far too young to be reading them. She loves sci-fi and fantasy worlds with strong, quirky heroines and hot, alpha males. When not writing, you can find her swooning over fictional love interests, binging angsty TV shows, or cuddling with her cute-but-demanding cats. She lives in Toronto, Canada.

She is the author of the *Bride to an Alien Prince* series, which was written with a co-author, and the forthcoming *Star-Marked Mates of Sollir* series. She was part of the *Claimed Among the Stars* anthology, which placed #42 on the USA Today Bestseller List in 2022.

Find Kate Online

Facebook:
@katestevensbooks
Instagram: @kstevensbooks
TikTok: @katestevensbooks
Pinterest:
@kstevensbooks
BookBub:
@kstevensbooks
Ko-fi: ko-fi.com/kstevensbooks
Website:
kstevensbooks.com

9 781990 551116